FINDING LARA

PJ FIALA

DEDICATION

I've had so many wonderful people come into my life and I want you all to know how much I appreciate it. From each and every reader who takes the time out of their days to read my stories and leave reviews, thank you. My beautiful, smart and fun Road Queens, who play games with me, post fun memes, keep the conversation rolling and help me create these captivating characters, places, businesses and more. Thank you ladies for your ideas, support and love.

The following characters and places were created by:

Glen Hollow - Kim Kurtz

Hickory Hills - Kathy Franklin

Matthew Vickers- Pamela Reveal

Lara Bennit - Kristi Hombs Kopydlowski

Keaton Bennit - Elinda Moody

Laylah Bennit - Yolanda Tobiasen

Lara's Delights - Anne Walker

Shianne Brown - Tjuana TJ Brown

Klaire Brown - Karen Cranford LeBeau

Troy Brown - Kristi Hombs Kopydlowski

Sheriff Rex Cranford - Karen Cranford LeBeau
Sharon Jackson - Belinda Jackson Hercule
Flynn DeMario - Terri DeMario
Millie LeBeau - Karen Cranford LeBeau
Divine Designs - Nicky Ortiz
Paxton's General Store - Abigail Capps
Employee at Paxton's - Alan - Julia Murphy
Hairy Beards - Barbershop Nathalie Juergensen
Homemade in the Hollow - Nancy Hoch
Chestnut Grove - Beckie Johnson Lowe
Bloomin' Lovely - Jo West
Porter's Steakhouse - Nicky Ortiz
Rayleigh Winters - Terra Oenning
Brookswood - Monique Mousseau Westwood
Baxter Fenshaw - Jo West
Fort Abraham - Amy Barber

BRR Black Road Resistance - Jamie Rogers
Everett Howard - Ronda Barnes-Howard
Craig Howard - Jayne Smith
Jasiah Weston - Jo West
Liam Price - Julie Ann Price
Cole Honeycutt - Ginna Honeycutt
Brayden Lowe - Beckie Johnson Lowe
Brock Harris - Sally Harris
Reece Mansfield - Lisa Mansfield
Kent -Mary Lou Melzer
Brenner Matthews - Karen Cranford LeBeau
Ramsey Stewart - Karen Cranford LeBeau

Last but not least, my family for the love and sacrifices
they have made and continue to make to help me achieve

this dream, especially my husband and best friend, Gene.
Words can never express how much you mean to me.
To our veterans and current serving members of our
armed forces, police and fire departments, thank you
ladies and gentlemen for your hard work and sacrifices;
it's with gratitude and thankfulness that I mention you in
this forward.

DESCRIPTION

He's a GHOST operative tasked with the impossible.

She's a small-town baker with the perfect blend of sweet and sass.

When Lara's abducted and Tate stops at nothing to get her back.

When the job can only be handled by the team that doesn't exist, you call GHOST.

For Tate Vickers, becoming a GHOST operative was inevitable. Being raised by GHOST operatives, he and his coworkers played rescue games as children. When he's tasked to run the elite group's satellite location in Kentucky, he jumps at the chance and brings his friends along. But Glen Hollow Kentucky, isn't what it seems. There's a dark secret living in the hills and a war is about to erupt.

Lara Bennit grew up baking in the kitchen of her best friend's mom. Now she bakes in her own and makes a respectable living doing what she loves. When local criminals break into her bakery and steal ingredients – repeatedly, her frustration grows. Then Tate walks into her small-town shop, and his presence is as comforting as the cinnamon rolls she just added to the bakery case. Maybe everything will be okay after all.

Or maybe her real problems are just beginning. And Tate is tasked with the ultimate job...

To Find Lara.

***

Let's stay in touch where bots and algorithms don't have a say in how we communicate.

My newsletter is where I share new book ideas, new releases, pre-orders and my friends offer my readers free books nearly every week. Sound like something you'd like? Join me here.

GLOSSARY - GHOST LEGACY

The kids from GHOST are all grown up and living lives of their own. Meet these men and women of GHOST Legacy.

Tate Vickers - Tate is the son of Gaige and Sophie Vickers. Their story is told in Defending Sophie. Tate is a recon specialist and runs the GHOST satellite office.

Aidyn Dunbar - Is the son of Bridget and Axel Dunbar. You can find their story is Defending Bridget. Aidyn specializes in sharpshooter and recon.

Spencer Lawson - Spencer is the son of Wyatt and Yvette Lawson. You can read their story in Defending Yvette. Spencer specialize's in security, recon and recovery.

Henry Delany - Henry is the son of Hawk and Roxanne Delany. Their story is told is Defending Roxanne. His specialties are recon, recovery, and anything that requires size.

Adelaide Masters - Adelaide's parents are Josh and Isabella Masters. Their story is told in Defending Isabella. Adelaide served in the Army and is the team's medic.

Maya Sager - Maya served in the US Marine Corps. Her parents are Dodge and Jax Sager. Their story is told in Finding His Jewel. Maya's specialty is recon and rescue.

Myles Sager - Myles served in the US Marine Corps. Myles and Maya are the twins of Dodge and Jax Sager. Myles is an explosives expert.

ONE

The sound of gunfire filled the air, and a bullet grazed the top of Tate Vickers's truck, just above his head.

"What the fuck?"

He ducked in the driver's seat as his eyes scanned the area all around him.

An older Ford pickup sped toward him, in his lane, and Tate gripped the steering wheel with both hands, ready to drive the ditch if need be.

He saw a flash of movement from his left up the narrow blacktop road, as an older Jeep Cherokee careened down the hill toward him.

The oncoming Ford sped past, followed closely by a squad car, lights on and siren blaring. The Jeep coming down the hill fell in line behind the squad car and Tate saw the driver reach his arm out the driver's window, a pistol in his hand.

Inhaling deeply, he slowed his truck, then spun it around in the road and followed the squad and company.

His teammates, who followed behind in their own vehicles, made the same U-turn and began pursuit with him.

Another bullet hit the top of his truck, though toward the passenger side. The driver of the Jeep had trained his weapon on Tate, though erratically, as his truck rambled along the road.

Gripping the steering wheel with both hands, Tate sped up and tapped the Jeep on the driver's side back bumper, then swerved to the left as the Jeep spun around to the right and hit the ditch. He'd loved practicing these PIT maneuvers in the military.

His teammates Henry Delany and Maya Sager stopped their vehicles behind the Jeep. They'd take care of bringing him in to the police station.

He now focused on the squad car in front of him chasing the older Ford truck. The truck turned sharply and sped up another blacktop road into the hills. The squad car in front of him slammed on his brakes, refusing to follow, and Tate had no choice but to swerve around it or explain himself later.

Bringing his truck to a stop a few yards ahead of the squad car, he tapped the call icon on his steering wheel and told the automated voice to call the Glen Hollow police department.

The dispatcher answered on the second ring. "Glen Hollow PD."

"This is Tate Vickers. I'm with GHOST and Fort Abraham. Just pulled into town amid a police chase involving guns. Please tell the police officer sitting alongside the road I'm a friendly and so are my coworkers."

"Hold on Mr. Vickers."

He waited in his truck and watched in his mirror to make sure his teammates were doing the same. He saw the officer in the car behind him talking on his phone and hoped that was dispatch calling. It gave him a moment to settle his nerves and calm his breathing.

The operator came back on the phone. "Mr. Vickers, Officer Bennit is aware you are friendly."

"Thank you."

He stepped from his truck, hands up in the air until Officer Bennit exited his vehicle and moved toward him.

"You can put your hands down, Mr. Vickers."

Lowering his hands, he nodded toward his teammates, and they exited their vehicles and walked toward them. He nodded at Officer Bennit. "Thank you. Why didn't you chase those men up the hill?"

"We have a treaty with them. We don't go up there. They aren't supposed to come down here."

"But they did, and they shot at you." He turned toward his truck. "And me. My truck sustained damage."

"I'm sorry, Mr. Vickers. Unfortunately, you were in the wrong place at the wrong time."

Tate's brows pinched together. This was unreal. "That's a fact. But you're going to just let them get away with that?"

"I don't have permission from the Town Council. It's something they must grant before I can go up there and speak to their president."

Tate looked up the hill where he could still hear engines gunning, realization dawning. "So those men are part of the Black Road Resistance?"

"Yes, sir."

Tate glanced at his teammates. His phone rang, and he looked at the readout to see that it was Maya.

"Hey, Maya."

"We have that asshole who shot at you."

"Okay, hang tight."

He pocketed his phone, then looked at Officer Bennit once again.

"My teammates have one of the Black Road Resistance men down the road."

Officer Bennit blew out a long breath and looked down the road. It curved and was impossible to see them from this location, but he stood for a long time looking down the road.

"They'll need to let him go."

"What?" Tate ran a hand through his hair. "You can't just let him go. The man shot at you. He fucking shot at me. He hit my truck and someone is going to have to pay for that."

Officer Bennit shook his head and turned to look him in the eye. "I know you think this is ludicrous, but I don't have jurisdiction to arrest them."

"Sir, it's a fact we're new here and have yet to learn how things work. But, there is no place on earth people can blindly shoot at others, especially police officers, and just walk away. What the hell is this all about?"

His teammates, Spencer Lawson, Aidyn Dunbar, and Adelaide Masters, stood around the officer, disbelief written on their faces plain as day.

Officer Bennit shrugged. "The sheriff will be setting up a town council meeting to discuss how to handle this latest round of activity from the BRR. They've been misbehaving lately and..." he shrugged. "It's complicated."

CHAPTER

TWO

Lara stood in the corner of her bakery and surveyed the damage. Flour and sugar were strewn all around. They had tossed the coffeemaker on the floor, pieces of broken coffee cups were scattered in the mess, and all she could think was that she didn't have time for this. And it was getting expensive.

She heard the sirens and gunshots outside and her stomach rumbled. Usually Clay Hollow was a quiet little town and the nicest place to live. But these past few weeks, it had been anything but. Now her father was out there chasing those jackasses and they were shooting at him. Afraid to walk to the window in case a stray bullet came through the large front window, a streak caught her attention, and tears immediately sprung to her eyes.

The lettering on her front window, Lara's Delights, her bakery's name painted on the big window and her door, were scraped through, a large gash in the paint distorting the name. Her name. She'd waited forever for the painter to come down from Lexington to paint her

9

door and front window. Those little bastards did more damage this time than they had in the past and she was sick and tired of dealing with it.

Her dad's squad car squealed to a stop outside. He rushed in and pulled her into his body for a big hug. She inhaled his musky scent and absorbed the warmth he offered because she needed it. Her body shook and her dad's arms tightened around her.

After a few minutes, he stepped back and looked into her eyes. His eyes were filled with concern.

"Honey, are you alright? Did they hurt you?"

"No." She shook her head. "I mean, yes, I'm alright and no, they didn't hurt me. But look what they did to my shop, Dad."

"We can clean the mess, honey."

"Again. You mean we can keep cleaning it over and over and I keep losing money? I feel very targeted here, Dad. This is the third time this month they've broken in here. Not that I want it to happen to others, but they have robbed no one else in town three times in a month."

She pointed to the writing in the flour on the floor. *"See ya soon."*

"Now they're taunting me. Those little fuckers."

"Lara!" He shook his head and swiped a hand down his jaw.

"I'm tired of this, Dad. I've done nothing to those little shits."

"We'll figure something out."

A white pickup truck pulled into her parking lot. She inhaled deeply and picked her way slowly across the slippery floor. She reached the door just as a tall, dark-haired man did. He pushed the door open and stepped inside, then looked around at the mess.

"I'm sorry. As you can see, I'm not open right now."

"I'm sorry about that. I actually stopped here because I saw Officer Bennit's squad car here and hoped to chat."

She turned to her dad. His jaw tightened, and he seemed less than pleased at this visitor.

"Hello, Mr. Vickers. This here is my daughter, Lara. This is her bakery." He nodded at her. "Honey, this is Tate Vickers. He's new in town. He and his teammates were hired to help with security at the base."

"Nice to meet you, Mr. Vickers. I wish you were here to help with security in town."

The corner of her father's mouth turned down, and she felt bad. Sort of. "Lara, honey…"

"Nope, Daddy, I'm sick of this shit."

Tate turned as he took in all the damage. "You mean those men in the trucks shooting at us did this?"

"They sure did, and this is the third time this month."

Tate looked at her dad. "Officer Bennit, my team and I are coming into the police station tomorrow morning to talk about what's going on here. It appears there is a lot to discuss. Are they breaking into all the businesses in town?"

Lara didn't let her father answer. "They've broken into the gun shop. They stole handguns, rifles, and a shit ton of ammunition. They've broken into the gas stations in town and stolen gas. They broke into the electronics store and stole a bunch of things from there. Though I don't know why. It's not like they have internet up there."

Tate smiled reassuringly at her. Her lungs tightened, making it hard to take a breath. Then he turned toward her father once again and stared. "Why?"

"I told you, I don't have jurisdiction."

Tate inhaled deeply, and she saw his impressive

muscular chest expand and stretch under the gray t-shirt he wore. Her eyes trailed down his arms and saw the muscles and veins, but she didn't trust herself to scan lower.

She turned toward her father once more and watched his face. It had been bugging her lately at how quiet he got when they talked about the BRR.

Shaking her head, she slowly made her way across the floor and stepped behind her bakery counter where she had set her cleaning supplies. "He won't talk about the BRR. He won't do anything about them either."

"Honey, I've told you, it's complicated."

"It sure as hell is, Daddy. 'Cause I'm going to carry my gun and if one of those little fuckers comes back here, you're going to need to come and get him with the hearse."

"Lara, don't do that. It'll start a war."

"They've started the war. This year they've been terrible while making their brew. It's intolerable and apparently, the folks who are here to help us..." She waved her hand in her father's direction, "don't have jurisdiction or, likely, the courage to do anything about those bastards."

"Lara..."

She held up her hand. "Nope. I don't want to hear anymore. I'm calling someone to install a security system and I'm going to catch them on camera. Then, I'm sending it to the governor and I'm going to cause such a stink here. They'll need to do something about this bullshit."

"I can help you with the security system." Tate said.

Tate pulled the speaker to the center of the dining room table in their rented house, but while they were here it was their office, conference room, and operations room. His five teammates sat around the table, laptops open.

His phone rang. "Vickers," he answered.

"Tate Vickers, I assume."

Tate grinned. "Yes, sir. I suppose I should have clarified."

"I knew who I was calling, Tate. My code name is Casper. That's all you'll ever know me by. I know your father has told you about our relationship and you know that my job here at the Department of Defense is top secret. But our relationship with GHOST over these past forty-plus years has benefitted us all and saved countless lives."

"Yes, sir. We're aware."

"Good. Please introduce yourselves, and just for fun, since I know you all have parents working with GHOST, tell me who your parents are so I can get a feel for who I'm working with on this team."

He looked around the table and nodded to Aidyn at his right.

"Sir, my name is Aidyn Dunbar, Bridget and Axel Dunbar are my parents. My specialty is sharpshooter and recon."

"Nice to meet you, Aidyn."

Tate nodded to Maya. "Sir, my name is Maya Sager. My parents are Jax and Dodge Sager. My specialty is recon and rescue."

Casper laughed on the other end of the line. "Ah yes, the indomitable Jax Sager. She's a spitfire for sure."

"Yes sir. Still is."

Casper chuckled again. "Nice to meet you, Maya."

Tate glanced at Spencer. "Spencer Lawson here, sir. My parents are Wyatt and Yvette Lawson. I specialize in security, recon, and recovery."

"Nice to meet you, Spencer."

"Adelaide Masters here. My parents are Josh and Isabella Masters. I'm the team's medic."

"Just like your mom."

"Yes, sir."

Tate grinned at Henry. "Last but not least..."

Henry gave him the finger but spoke to Casper. "Henry Delany, sir. Hawk and Roxanne Delany are my parents. My specialties are recon, recovery, and anything that requires size."

His comrades around the table laughed, and Casper chuckled. "Built like your father?"

"Yes, sir."

"Nice to have you all aboard and ready to help us here in Glen Hollow. I'll begin with what we're dealing with here. There is a group of people living up in the hills just south of Glen Hollow. They've dubbed their encampment Hickory Hills. They call themselves the Black Road Resistance and they believe themselves to be sovereign of the United States government and our laws. Back around sixty years ago when they defected and moved up into the hills, there was an all-out war. Over one hundred people perished during that time. To stop the bloodshed, the Mayor of Glen Hollow at the time entered into a truce with the president of the Black Road Resistance. This truce stated that the Black Road Resistance could live up in Hickory Hills without interference from the citizens of Glen Hollow, as long as they left the citizens alone. Mostly, it's been a truce that both parties have obeyed."

Tate looked around the table at his team, some typing into their computers, some staring at the speaker, and Henry looking out the window behind Maya.

Henry then asked, "What's changed, sir?"

"A few things. The new mayor in Glen Hollow has decided enough is enough. The Black Road Resistance distills an elixir every fall. This is the only type of currency they have. They will trade it for supplies for the next batch. Sugar is the biggest component they need that they don't have up there. They distill it down to make their elixir. The mayor has put a stop to that, telling the townspeople if they trade with the Black Road Resistance, there will be large fines."

Maya leaned forward. "Why do the townspeople trade for the elixir?"

"Apparently it's a potent drug that will help with breathing issues, even a heart malady or so, and you can also get quite high from it. But, in moderation, it has great benefits. We have scientists testing this elixir and applying it to a myriad of experiments to explore its benefits and its drawbacks. The BRR needs the money this year because their extension on the sixty-year deferment for the taxes on the land they're on has been denied by the town council at the mayor's urging. This means they can lose their land if they don't pay the taxes."

Tate's team nodded their heads.

Casper continued. "Also, as you know, we've begun building the new military installation on the southeast side of town. The Resistance has thwarted or tried to thwart our construction company's efforts. Currently, communication lines are being installed. The night before last, the Resistance blew up the connector box with homemade Molotov cocktails. Our workers don't feel safe there and they're hampering our ability to get the base built on time. We need your expertise in managing the damage and keeping the BRR from hampering our progress. The base must be built. We are making plans to move troops onto the facility by spring next year."

Tate glanced at his teammates once again and saw them nodding in agreement. "Yes sir. We understand and will do what's needed to accomplish this."

"You work for me. Not the mayor, no matter how he may try to make you think otherwise. Personally, I wish he hadn't stirred up this mess with the Resistance, but it's been done and now we have to clean up the fallout."

"Yes sir. We understand. If the treaty was working, why is the mayor taking a hard stance on the BRR?"

"All we've been told was he lost family members in the war with them sixty years ago. He's harbored a hatred of the treaty and the BRR since then. You'll find the town divided. Half say let them be, as long as they're good, the other half wants to chase them off the land and get them out of there." Casper cleared his throat and finished the meeting with, "I know you'll do a great job. Call me if you need anything."

The line went dead, and they stared at it for a moment, then looked at each other.

Tate heaved out a breath. "So that bakery robbery yesterday was for the sugar. I'm going to go see if Lara had refused to trade with them, and that further angered them."

Aidyn stood and pulled his cap up on his head, "Is that why you're going over there?"

Maya laughed. "He has a sweet tooth, you know."

Spencer stood as well and closed the lid on his laptop.

"Spencer, I told Lara Bennit we could install a security system at her place."

"You told her WE could install a system?" Spencer laughed, and so did his teammates.

"Yes. I'll help you. Before we head over to the base later for our meeting, I'd like to get one installed. They've targeted her place, likely for the sugar she has. But she's sick of it and wants to capture these thieves on camera. Her father is Officer Bennit. As you can see, he's doing nothing to help her."

Spencer chuckled. "I'll be back down with the system."

FOUR

Lara heaved the large plastic bag from the can. The broken cups and glasses rattled as she plopped it on the floor and tied the top together. Her dad stepped into the kitchen with her. "I'll take that, honey. I'm sure it's heavy with all that's in it."

"Thanks, Dad." Glancing at the big black and white clock on the wall above the sink, she stretched her shoulders. "It's almost lunchtime. Can I make you something to eat?"

"No, honey, your mom needs me at home to make her lunch, and I feel better when I know she's had her medicine."

She stepped from the kitchen and surveyed her bakery. "What medicine is she on Dad? You change the subject each time I ask."

Her dad kissed her temple and lifted the bag. Watching as he carried the garbage out the back door, she inhaled deeply. Her parents and their secrets were a sore spot with her.

The bell on the front door announced a visitor. She looked up and stared at none other than Tate Vickers.

"Hi. I'm sorry, but I'm still not open for business."

He smiled at her. Smiled. It was the most beautiful smile she'd ever seen. Yesterday, she'd noticed that he was attractive. But her mind was clearly not working right yesterday because she didn't remember him looking this handsome.

"Actually, I have a couple of questions to ask you, if you don't mind."

"Why do you have questions?"

Tate looked around at her bakery. She watched him grin when his eyes landed on the little tables with the tabletops painted in bright, cheery colors. She'd painted them herself and her dad had glass tops made for each one to protect the paint. Luckily, only one of them broke in the melee.

"I can't help but wonder if the reason they targeted your bakery is that they want the sugar. I've heard the BRR needs it to make their elixir."

She cocked her head to the left and studied his face. It was a pleasant face. He had dark hair, and though he'd combed it back earlier in the day, some of it had fallen over his forehead. The length in the back curled at the collar of his shirt. The sides had a nice wave and though it was dark, she could see shades of golds and reds where the sun highlighted them.

She rubbed her lips together, the taste of the gloss she'd applied a while ago still present. The back door opened then closed and Tate's dark brown eyes lifted above her head, searching for the source of the sound. She heard her father's footsteps behind her crunch on the floor, still covered in flour and sugar.

"Well, hello, Tate. How are you finding Glen Hollow?"

Tate inhaled. "Well, it was certainly exciting enough in the beginning, but last night was peaceful."

She stepped back and to the side to see her father, and he nodded. "Yes, I'm sorry your first minutes in town were such as they were. Normally, ours is a peaceful little town."

She scoffed. "It hasn't been peaceful for the past month, Dad. Those BRR kids have been hellions." She turned to Tate. "The last two times they broke in, they stole sugar, which, as you've stated, is what they need for their elixir. This time, they wrecked the place for good measure."

Tate's eyes stared into hers. "Why do you think they broke things and damaged the bakery?"

"My best guess is that I told them I wouldn't trade with them anymore. I've told them that several times. I guess they don't like the answer."

His brows bunched, then smoothed. "They could have hurt you. It doesn't appear they like the confrontation."

"I don't care. I'm sick of them coming here and the sheriff, and"—she looked at her father—"my dad, refuses to do anything about it. They won't go up in the hills and talk to their president. It's infuriating."

Tate's eyes darted to her father, and she saw it. Her dad flinched and his shoulders dropped.

"Honey, you know we can't do that. We have a truce with them."

"They've broken the truce. But look at what they've been doing all around town. The base has suffered too."

Her father glanced at Tate and she turned her head to

watch Tate's reaction. "That's why we're here. We plan to secure the installation so they can make progress. They'd like to get back on track."

"What are you, security guards?"

His cheeks tinted pink, and she changed her mind about how handsome he was. He was stunning.

"Not exactly, but sort of."

"Well, that makes things clear as mud."

Tate opened his mouth to say something, but her father interrupted. "I think things will settle down now. They'll likely know we won't tolerate them shooting at our citizens. But I have no choice except to leave this up to the town council. They have a town hall meeting scheduled for tomorrow night."

Tate addressed her father. "Why do you think things have escalated?"

"The mayor has taken a hard line on locals exchanging with them. While some store owners still do, others have refused." He shrugged. "It's angered them. Along with the building of Fort Abraham, and the fact that their sixty-year tax deferment on the land isn't being renewed this year, it's set them off. Plus, you know how teens are. Those youngsters haven't been reined in yet."

Tate looked at her. "When did you first refuse to exchange with them?"

"A month ago. I'll continue to as well." She huffed out a breath and rotated her head. A headache was coming on for sure.

"Spencer is right behind me. We'll get your security system set up today."

"Really? We didn't talk about cost."

"I can eat a lot of cookies."

"Only cookies? I think that security equipment may be expensive and cookies doesn't pay for the equipment."

"I'll worry about the materials. You bake cookies."

FIVE

She was a spitfire. He certainly thought she was pretty too, but man, that spunk.

Her father's phone rang, and he stepped out the back door.

Tate waited for the door to close. "Why do you think they won't do anything to those kids?"

She turned to face him, then bit her bottom lip.

"I don't know. It's the strangest thing. And it's been bothering the hell out of me. Last year, when they came down, Dad was all hot and bothered about stopping them. He and the sheriff had dozens of meetings with the mayor. Then, one day, it was like a switch flipped."

"But he said the mayor drew a hard line. It seems like the mayor would just tell them to go up there and arrest them."

She shook her head. "They'd never do that. It would be an all-out war."

His brows furrowed. "Weapons were drawn, it appears war has started."

"Yeah. I guess."

He looked out the window, which offered him a view of the base of Hickory Hill. "So last year they weren't as bad as this year?"

"No. That's when things got weird. The new kid came down. I'd never seen him before. My dad stopped him while he was speeding through town about two months ago. I thought it was about time. But Dad didn't give him a ticket, and he did nothing else either. And, since then, he's been quiet about it all."

Tate chuckled. "Does he have some blackmail on your dad?"

Her head cocked to the right, and she stared into his eyes for a while longer than was comfortable. But he didn't look away. "I have thought that. The way things changed. But I can't imagine what it could be."

The back door opened, and Keaton Bennit carefully entered the bakery. "I have to run. The Sheriff is asking for a meeting before the town hall meeting. I understand you and your team will be around right after lunch."

Tate nodded, "Yes, sir. We'll be there."

Keaton stepped into the room further and kissed Lara on the temple. "I'll stop by later, Lara. Don't stay too late, with them boys as wild as they are right now."

"If you'd arrest them, none of us would have to worry about them."

"Don't start again, honey. I've got enough to deal with."

He waved to them both and disappeared through the doorway leading to the back.

Tate looked around once again. "Do you need help with anything?"

She chuckled. "You offering to help me clean?"

Shrugging, "Yeah. I guess. I mean, I have a little time before Spencer gets here."

She turned and grabbed a new garbage bag and lined the empty can. "It's almost as if I've fallen into an alternate universe."

He laughed. "You don't believe in that stuff, do you?"

"No, but it would explain a lot of things these days."

"I'll give you that." He walked to the far side of the bakery and picked up a couple of the colorful chairs laying on their sides. Finding a broom against the wall, he began sweeping the floor and Lara walked behind the bakery counter and pulled all the baked goods from inside and tossed them in the garbage can.

"It makes me sad to see all that going to waste."

"Me too. But I can't risk that broken glass or debris didn't touch them. Plus, with the dust we've been stirring up with the sweeping and the flour filling the air, they won't taste the same. I'll start fresh in the morning."

"How early are you going to start?"

She tossed a pan of cookies into the garbage and shrugged. "Around two or three a.m. I guess."

He shook his head, and his phone rang.

"Vickers."

"Mr. Vickers, this is Baxter Fenshaw. I'm a construction manager at Fort Abraham. I'd like to change our meeting from later this afternoon to two thirty today."

"I think we can make that work, Mr. Fenshaw."

"Baxter. Call me Baxter. I'll see you then. Come to the construction office on the grounds. I'll wait for you here."

"Confirmed."

Spencer's truck rolled to a stop near the front door.

Tate stood his broom against the wall and turned to help Spencer bring in the camera equipment. Lara stopped tossing items into the garbage and glanced out the window.

"I think we need to discuss payment again, Tate."

"Look, we have the equipment, and you need it. We can always order more if we need to. Let's just say we'll install it. If you like it in a few months, we'll talk about payment. If you don't like it, you can find another system you prefer, and we'll take ours out."

Her smile was small, tentative, and nervous. But Spencer entered the bakery, stalling any further discussion of payment.

"Holy shit. They did a number here."

Lara brushed her hands together. "It was worse. Believe it or not, I've cleaned some of this up. But I focused on the kitchen first, so out here took a backseat."

"Okay. Shit." Spencer looked his way.

"Do you mind helping me carry in the cameras?"

"Not at all."

He glanced at Lara and nodded, then headed out the door to Spencer's truck. He swallowed the lump in his throat and filled his lungs with air.

Spencer lowered the tailgate on his truck and pulled the totes filled with equipment toward them. Tate grabbed the first one as Spencer pulled his toolbox off the tailgate. They walked in silence toward the door. Just before opening it, Spencer chuckled. "She's pretty."

"Yes, she is."

"I didn't expect to find hot chicks here, but it sure is looking up."

Tate swallowed again and shrugged off the heat that

filled his gut. What did he care if Spencer liked Lara? They could both date whoever they wanted.

"Yeah. I guess."

Spencer scoffed and Tate sauntered past him with the boxy tote he carried. "Where's your office, Lara?"

She hesitated for a fraction, then shook her head and pointed to a small door across from the kitchen.

Pushing one of her colorful tables into place, Lara stepped back as her front door opened. Whirling around, she stared into the face of her smiling best friend, Shianne.

"Hi!" She threw her arms around her friend's shoulders. "I'm so happy to see you."

"I'm sorry I couldn't get here earlier, but work was a bear today."

"How can that be? Is there a rush on clothing or something?"

Shianne shook her head. "I hope you didn't forget about the Bourbon Ball in two weeks. I've had to keep a list of dresses ladies have purchased, so no two are the same. Mrs. Hopkins came in today and looked at five dresses that others have already purchased. She insisted on knowing who purchased the dresses ahead of her and when I wouldn't give out the information, she chewed me a new one. Man, she was mad. In the end, she found a dress she seemed happy with, but good gawd, she was angry."

"Didn't you have problems with Mrs. Hopkins last year? Next year, you need to call her a month ahead and remind her to come in."

"I did that this year and she waited until today!" Shianne looked around the bakery, and her shoulders slumped. "I'm so sorry, Lara. I can't believe they've done this."

She let out a breath, and her shoulders slumped, too. "I know." She looked at the front of the bakery, then to her friend. "Look what they did to my window."

Shianne turned, then gasped as her hands flew to cover her mouth. "Oh no! You waited so long for that to be painted."

"Yeah. They've cut to the core this time."

"Why? I don't understand why. You didn't trade with them last year either."

"I know. I've run that through my head over and over. There are a couple of new boys or men or whatever they are, this year. I've not seen them before. Dad says they're sewing their wild oats, but yesterday they shot at Dad and Tate."

"I heard. It was all anyone would talk about today. Aren't they going to do anything about that?"

"I haven't spoken to my dad since his meeting with the mayor today."

Shianne pulled her into a warm embrace, and she soaked up the love she felt coming through. "Thank you," she whispered.

Shianne giggled. "Of course, silly." They pulled apart, and Shianne clapped her hands together. "So, tell me about Tate."

"There's really nothing to tell. He and his teammates

are in town to help with security at the base. They installed a security system here earlier today, too."

"Really? Gosh, the gossip mongers didn't mention that today."

"It's likely they didn't know. It came about late yesterday when Tate stopped in to speak to my dad. Then this morning, he and Spencer came in and installed it. They were only here around an hour."

"It appears you're getting to know them pretty well."

"Not really. And don't get any big ideas."

Shianne giggled. "Okay, put me to work."

"Sadly, I was just about to mop the floors. It'll probably take two or three washes to get all the flour off the floor."

"I'm your girl. I'm a great mopper."

"Thank you, Shianne. I'll get into the kitchen and begin making the bread dough so it can rise overnight. I've already mopped and cleaned the entire kitchen."

"You poor dear. Didn't anyone come and help you?"

"My mom isn't feeling well again, and Dad had his meeting so…"

"What's your mom's ailment this time?"

"Your guess is as good as mine. Once again, Dad won't say a word."

"Oh boy." Shianne clapped her hands once more. "I'm here now. You go do what you do—bake. I'll clean up the sales floor."

"Will do."

Shianne picked up the bucket she'd used to mop the kitchen and headed toward the sink in the utility room. "What are you wearing to the Bourbon Ball? You haven't come in yet for your dress."

"I don't know if I'm going. With all of this going on,

I'll be extending my hours to make up for the expense of all of this until my insurance checks get to me."

"You have to go, Lara. We've never missed a year."

"Who are you going with? You haven't said."

She shrugged her shoulder. "I don't think I have a date this year."

"What?" She poked her head out of the kitchen and looked across the hall at the utility room, where Shianne filled the mop bucket with water.

"I know. It's getting kind of bad here. I know nearly every male in town and I'm not interested in any of them. I've either graduated with the eligibles, or I've known them my entire life. Or, they're my parents' age."

"Yeah. I guess."

"So what does this Tate look like?"

Lara stared at her friend, and the feeling of jealousy knotted her stomach faster than she cared to admit. "He's handsome. Tall and muscular. His hair rolls up in the back and touches his collar. It looks soft. He has a pleasant smile and dark brown eyes. He has a sexy voice, too."

Shianne laughed out loud. "For such a nonchalant response to your meeting, you sure noticed a lot about him."

Lara inhaled a deep breath, then smiled at her friend. "Mop." She re-entered the kitchen and mentally planned what she needed to make first. First, she'd make some cookies and while they cooled, she'd get her bread started, then she'd plan her muffins and pastries. But, before any of that could be done, she needed to get more flour, sugar, and other ingredients, thanks to the BRR. Man, she was sick of them.

She pulled her phone from her back pocket and

opened the app for Paxton's General Store. It had been a tiny mom-and-pop shop back in the day, but since their son had taken over, they'd modernized. Somewhat. Hopefully, they'd still deliver today.

She filled out her order and held her breath when she sent it in. A message came back to her they would deliver her order in an hour. Letting out an enormous sigh of relief, she pulled out the ingredients she had on hand and prepared as much as she could until her order arrived.

Just as she lifted the sugar she'd hidden behind boxes on the bottom shelf, she heard the gunning of an engine outside and dread filled her body as she associated the sounds of trouble coming.

The brief pit stop at Lara's Delights to install the security system was a nice way to get back into working. They'd been off for four days, mostly to make the move here to Glen Hollow. And to get themselves situated before they got busy working around the clock at the construction site. But they weren't the resting kind, and he found the time off stressed him out more than revived and invigorated him. Note to self: four days off is too many. Thank goodness he'd had some distractions, like getting shot at, though that wasn't a pleasant distraction. And installing a security system at Lara's Delights.

Pulling onto the base property, he and his passengers, Spencer and Henry, inspected the area. He noticed heavy equipment, piles of dirt, and stacks of building materials. The workers were gone from the site and they were to meet the general manager, Baxter Fenshaw.

"Look around for the construction office."

Henry was the first to see it. "It's to the right by the gigantic tree."

The faded yellow trailer was parked under the largest tree on the grounds at this point. Made sense; it was a likely a hot box out here during the day. He glanced in the mirror and saw the dust whirling around behind him, obscuring their other teammates.

He pulled his truck to a stop in front of the trailer and waited while the dust settled.

A robust man emerged from the trailer and stood on the metal steps leading up to the door. His enormous hands were tucked up to the second knuckle in his front pockets. His white hair gleamed in the sunshine, his tanned face a stark contrast to his light hair.

Tate stepped from his truck and his teammates followed suit as they approached the man, who he assumed was Fenshaw.

He held his hand out as he neared the top step, their boots clomping up the metal stairs. "Tate Vickers."

The man grabbed his hand in a firm grip and pumped it enthusiastically. "Baxter Fenshaw. Nice to meet you." He stepped aside and motioned toward the door. "Please go on in, it's cooler in there."

Tate entered the trailer first and listened as each teammate introduced themselves to Baxter.

The room was what he'd call organized chaos. There were plans laid out on a long table against the far wall and others pinned to the wall above it. Photographs and drawings were stuck to the wall in various places, depicting the finished product.

The room filled with the seven of them, but there were chairs at the back of the long room and his team-mates found their seats at Baxter's urging.

"Now then." He sat behind the old wooden desk and moved stacks of papers. Tate took the chair directly in front of the desk but moved it aside, so his teammates could see Baxter. "I'm not sure what information you've received, and I've heard that you met the worst of the BRR yesterday." Baxter leveled his gaze at him. "Looks like your truck took some heat."

"Yes, sir."

"I've got the name of a garage that'll do good work for you."

"Thank you. I appreciate that."

"We've begun construction on the communications infrastructure. We laid pipe and pulled wires only to have them sons-a-bitches blow it up. They didn't blow all of it up and we've now repaired or replaced most of what they damaged. But I believe they'll do it again."

Maya scooted forward in her chair. Her long dark hair pulled up in her usual ponytail. She was slight of frame, one of the most mentally strong people he knew. "Why are they focusing on the base?"

Baxter grinned at her, then frowned. "For some strange reason, they believe they own this land. Claim they've owned it for years."

"I thought they owned the mountain they call Hickory Hills."

Baxter grabbed a rolled-up map standing in the corner behind his desk and spread it out in front of him. "If you'd all like to come over here, I'll show you what they think. At least as near as I can tell."

Tate and his teammates all stood and gathered around the desk. He and Maya scooted behind the desk next to Baxter to make room.

Baxter pointed to the hill on the map. "This is Hickory Hill. That's what they named it. Its actual name, back in the day, was Sugar Maple Mountain. It's the largest population of the sugar maple, which is what the BRR use for their elixir. But they wanted control of it and nothing to do with anything the US decided, and that also meant the name."

They nodded, and Baxter continued. His finger slid down the map to the base of the mountain. "This is where we are. They've decided that since this property starts on the other side of this road," his finger drew along the bottom of the mountain, "that this is theirs and by extension, so is the rest of this property. The mayor has asked them for documentation as to their ownership and they've provided none."

Adelaide stood directly in front of Baxter. She and Maya were similar enough to look like sisters. "How did they get ownership of the mountain to begin with?"

"Great question, Adelaide. Sixty years ago, when Everett Howard Sr. led his folks up the mountain and started the war that led to them defecting and setting up residence there, his father owned that land up there. Though they've not paid the taxes in those sixty years due to a tax deferment. Now that the town council has decided to call the deferment, the mood is changing. If it comes to the town actually going up there to remove them, it will be bloody. The people are tough. They live on the land. They hunt and build their own homes and structures with rudimentary equipment, and they have a hardened edge to them from years of built-up hate toward the townspeople. This is largely why they've let them be all these years. So, they believe because Everett's father had a deed, they have a deed. And that may be true, but legally, it hasn't been tended to."

Aidyn pointed at the map. "But the road is only about two feet on this side of the mountain."

"That's the truth. But, when the war settled and the state of Kentucky let them have the mountain, they claimed their boundaries were the black roads that led to the mountain roads. Black Road Resistance. Since this black road is on their land, no matter what the survey says, they are claiming it. It feels like another war is about to break out over it."

Tate took in a deep breath. "You don't look old enough to have been alive during the first war with the resistance. But have you heard all the stories?"

"All my life. My father lost a hand in that war. My uncles all fought in it. There is bitterness down here as much as up there. But, as time has gone on, life has improved for us down here. Life has largely stayed the same up there. At least as far as we can tell."

"So, no one goes up there?"

"No. That's the rule."

Henry crossed his arms over his chest. "Why do they come down here if that's the rule?"

"They brew their elixir at the end of September through the middle of October. They asked nicely and were granted permission for a couple of their members to come down and trade their elixir for supplies. Sometimes that's gas for their four-wheelers and motors. Sometimes that's sugar and other products they need to brew. Sometimes it's material and supplies for making clothing. But building this military facility has really stirred them up. Plus, the current president, Everett Howard, Jr., is in his late sixties and rumor has it his son, Craig Howard, is chomping at the bit to become president."

Tate tucked his thumbs in his front pockets. "So that's how they're organized. president, vice president, etc. And how are those positions filled?"

Baxter leaned back in his chair and sighed. "Father to son, to son, etc. The Howard family will do anything to stay in control of the resistance. And, if you care to know my opinion, Craig Howard is much more volatile than his father."

L ara placed the third batch of decorated cookies in the glass case in the bakery store front and smiled. They looked lovely. The bakery smelled heavenly, as usual, and every surface was cleaned and polished until it shined.

She glanced briefly at the wall clock. five more minutes until she unlocked her door. A vehicle pulled into her parking lot, the headlights sweeping across the store, and she held her breath for a moment. "Please be a customer and not a BRR jerk," she muttered.

She laid her hand on her tummy and swallowed a few times. Stepping toward the door, she saw the white truck in the parking lot, its headlights now turned off. The top of the truck had two bullet holes in it, and she recognized Tate in the driver's seat, talking to someone on the phone.

Her lips quivered slightly, and she unlocked her front door, then stepped back to flip the light switches on the wall near the kitchen door. She tugged the chain on her "open" sign and watched as Tate glanced up at her. They stared for a few seconds and her tummy flipped again. This time was a different flip, though.

Stepping behind her bakery case, proud of how it looked this morning, she checked the coffeepot and started another one. Soon the morning coffee drinkers would flow in, and she was excited to be ready.

The door opened, the doorbell Tate had set up for her rang, and there he stood.

"Good morning."

He smiled his dreamy smile at her. "Good morning. The place looks fantastic."

"Thank you. Shianne and I worked until eleven last night cleaning it up."

"Who's Shianne?"

"Oh, she's my best friend. She owns a clothing boutique in town, Divine Designs."

"Okay. I'll let Maya and Adelaide know, if they haven't found it yet."

"Maya and Adelaide?"

He chuckled. "My teammates. Though, I'll say upfront, they aren't super girly. Maya is just like her mom and a tomboy through and through. Adelaide is a bit more girly, but not overly so and I don't know if I can remember either of them ever saying they'd shopped. Much less in a boutique. But, never say never."

She nervously laughed. "Maybe they'll shop for dresses for the Bourbon Ball."

"The Bourbon Ball? We don't know what that is."

She took a deep breath. "It's a dressy ball we have each year in town here. Always the last Saturday in September and all the money goes to charities. It's called the Bourbon Ball because the local distilleries initially started it and they donate the most money to it. They also ply all ball attendees with plenty of delicious bourbon to keep them inebriated well into Sunday."

Tate laughed. "Okay, sounds like fun." He tucked his thumbs into his front pockets and looked at the glass case and the delicious baked goods she had inside. "You must have been baking for hours."

"Yes. I started yesterday afternoon while Shianne was out here cleaning."

"It shows."

He leaned closer to the glass and studied her cookies. She'd spent extra time on them because she wanted today's goods to stand out. She'd come back from a burglary, and she was strong.

"You do a fantastic job decorating. Wow, those are too pretty to eat."

She chuckled. "Good lord, I hope not. I'll go out of business if that's the case."

"Point taken. I'll take the blue one that looks like a present. The white front door cookie and the dog cookie."

She pulled on a glove, opened a white paper bakery bag and gently set his cookies inside. "How about coffee?"

"Yes ma'am. I'm going to need it. Today's my first day out at the base."

"Are you working in shifts out there?"

"Yes. We drew cards for the shifts and I'm lucky. Aidyn too. He's already on his way out there. But I wanted to come in and see that things were going alright for you and, as I said, I love cookies."

She giggled and poured him a cup of coffee. "Cream

and sugar are down there." She pointed to the counter. At the end of the glass case were a variety of creamers and sugars.

He added a bit of creamer to his coffee and snapped the lid on top. Reaching back for his wallet, he pulled out a twenty and handed it over to her.

Shaking her head, she refused his money. "Nope. You said I'd pay you for the security system with cookies, and that's what I'm doing."

"I said, if you liked it, we'd talk about price in a few months."

She smiled at him and enjoyed the smile he returned. "I'll keep track of the cookies you eat, and we'll go from there."

His grin grew larger. "Fair enough." He walked to the end of the counter again and pulled a wooden stir stick from the holder. "Have a great day, Lara. I hope your first day open after the break-in is the best one yet."

"Thank you, Tate. I hope your first day at the base is your best one yet." He halted and his head cocked. "No wait. I didn't mean that. I mean, I hope your first day at the base is fantastic." She inhaled deeply and felt her cheeks heat.

"Thanks, Lara. See you later."

He sauntered out of the bakery, and she watched him. Every step. The man had a nice behind. He had a nice front, too. He... boy, she was inept at summoning coherent thoughts at the moment. Lack of sleep was a real thing. She meant he was handsome. Probably she shouldn't talk much today, just smile and nod a lot.

Tate's headlights bounced off her walls as he pulled from the parking lot, and she watched as his truck drove away.

She strode to the end of the counter to straighten the creamers and saw the twenty-dollar bill laying under the creamer container. She instinctively looked out the window and shook her head. How to handle this?

NINE

This job was far from the usual, and he suspected that during the day, there'd be very little to do. Which he wasn't looking forward to.

The sun was just peeking over the horizon, shrouding the hills in a gorgeous orange-yellow light. "What do you think we should do while we're here during the day, Tate?" Aidyn asked.

He grinned. "I was just thinking about that. While Spencer's here, he can work with the communications team and learn what they're up to. Not that he doesn't already have a ton of knowledge, but this is an enormous job. So, different skill set." He glanced around. "So we don't go insane from boredom, we could work with the construction company and help with the building. We'd still be here if the BRR come down."

"I wouldn't mind some physical work."

"First thing we should do is familiarize ourselves with the plans. Let's hike the entire perimeter today. Then we could target practice, or we could run through some recon exercises, too."

Aidyn shrugged. "I'm on board with all of that."

"Great. Let's check in with Baxter first, then we'll look at what we need to do for today."

They walked up the metal steps to the door of the construction office. Lights glowed from the windows and the aroma of coffee wafted outside. He knocked, then heard Baxter's gruff voice call out, "Come in."

Tate twisted the knob on the door and entered the trailer. Baxter stood at the window next to his desk and stared out into the darkness, his phone pressed to his ear.

"Yeah, they just walked in. I'll send them over."

Baxter tapped his phone and tossed it on his desk.

"So, those BRR bastards came down last night and cut up our wires. All that we'd just repaired, they cut it all up. I've got my guys taking pictures and waiting for the sheriff to arrive. I'm on my way to see the damage for myself. You may as well come with me. I want you to see if you can find tracks and what they used to snip the wires. They're large in diameter, no regular tool would cut them, unless they took their time to cut through the casing first and then the individual wires inside."

Tate nodded and glanced at Aidyn. They both followed Baxter from the trailer. Baxter stomped to a dirty white pickup truck a few yards from Tate's truck. "You may as well bring your own truck. I'll need to come back here to handle the other issues from last night."

Tate pointed to his truck. "I'll drive Aidyn, hop in."

Aidyn grinned. "Maybe day shift won't be as boring as we feared it would be."

"So far, so good."

He climbed into his truck and took another drink from his coffee. Aidyn climbed in and looked in the white bakery bag sitting on the console. "So you stopped by Lara's Delights this morning."

"Yep. She makes great cookies."

Aidyn laughed, pulled his seatbelt across his body and clicked it in place. Tate backed his truck from its parking space and turned toward the construction site at large and waited for Baxter to lead the way.

"How bad do you think it's going to get here?" Aidyn asked.

"I can't imagine. But it sure seems the townspeople are gearing up for an all-out war. If they keep fucking with the base, though, they'll find their diplomatic immunity rescinded in a heartbeat."

"That's what I was thinking." Aidyn ran his hands down his face and yawned.

"Did you sleep last night?"

"Not that great." Aidyn stretched his shoulders. "New bed. Unknown place. Unfamiliar noises. I hope Spencer gets our security system in place today. It'll help us all sleep better if we don't have to listen to every little noise."

Tate chuckled. "That's the truth right there."

The construction site was laid out with nothing but the footings poured. The main building seemed massive. There were several buildings situated around the main building. According to the plans Baxter had shown them yesterday, they'd start with these first eight buildings and add more as it became fully operational.

They laid the main communication infrastructure in the main building and running under the basement area. Baxter's pickup came to a stop in front of the main building and Tate pulled in alongside him. They exited the trucks and Tate couldn't help but look down into the basement of the main building. Massive was an understatement.

There were a few men standing in the basement looking over a broken PVC pipe. Temporary stairs were situated to his right. He nodded to Aidyn and pointed to them, and both headed down to the basement of the main building.

The heat dissipated the further down they went, and he had to admit, it felt good. They neared the group of men and looked into the shallow well in the cement reserved for the wiring harnesses. The PVC pipe was smashed with a hammer or other heavy object, and someone had snipped individually the wires but not neatly. They were tugged and pulled in different directions, and it looked to be a mess.

Baxter came to stand near him, and the men stepped back for him to view the damage. His face was unusually red today, and Tate feared he'd have a heart attack if it directly related to stress.

Baxter glanced at Aidyn and him, then casually said, "This is Tate Vickers and Aidyn Dunbar, who are here to keep the BRR off our backs."

The men nodded or offered greetings, but they each waited for Baxter's next words nervously.

Baxter knelt by the largest grouping of cut wires, then glanced over at the next grouping and shook his head.

"Finish getting the pictures taken and wait for the sheriff. We'll need to rerun all these wires."

Baxter started toward the stairs and muttered. "Get your security guy out here and install cameras. Then, I think we're going to need to discuss your schedules and how we can all work together. I can't have any more delays. Especially not because of those bastards."

TEN

She'd call today a success. Yep, a total success. Sometimes it wasn't the worst thing having people rally around to help you when you've been the victim of some horrible, stupid thing. So, the towns-folk came out in droves and the only downside about it all was that she now had to stay here for a few hours to replenish the sales case.

It was a labor of love. She'd always loved baking. It's what made her open this bakery. But her shoulders ached, and her feet throbbed. Today was one of those days she wished she had a helper. She ran all day long. She bent down to wipe the crumbs from the bottom of the bakery case and spread out the few things she had left inside until she could replenish.

The bell on her door chimed, and she glanced up to see Tate walk in with another man.

"Hi." She stood. "I have little left, I'm afraid."

His smile was pleasant. He had the nicest smile, and it reached his eyes. They creased at the corners and added character to his handsome face. Not that he didn't have character anyway, but this was a lovely touch. Genuine is the word she'd use.

"I'd guess today was a tremendous success for you then."

"It was. Folks I haven't seen in a long time showed up to support me."

"That's the great thing about a small town." He turned his head to his friend. "Lara, this is Aidyn, one of my teammates."

"Hi, Aidyn, it's nice to meet you."

"Nice to meet you too, Lara. Tate says you bake the best cookies he's ever tasted and since he wouldn't share with me, I asked him to stop on the way home to pick up more."

She tsked and shook her head. "It's not nice to not share."

Tate shrugged and grinned. His cheeks tinted a cute pink. "That's why we're here. I'm buying for the house tonight. What do you have left? We'll bring something back for everyone."

She chuckled. "I have four banana nut muffins. A half dozen sugar cookies and one apple pie left."

"We'll take it."

"All of it?"

"Yep. What we don't eat tonight, we'll have for breakfast."

She pulled a bakery bag from the holder under the counter and opened it. They watched her work, and it made her nervous, but she'd done this a million times before. After filling the bag, she pulled the pie from the case behind her and set it in the pie box and folded in the corners. She laid it on the counter before them, then pulled her phone out and used the calculator.

"You left far too much money this morning, and I'm adding this to what I'll owe you for the security system."

"Lara..."

"You gentlemen have a fantastic night now."

Tate grinned broadly, and Aidyn laughed. "We've been dismissed, Tate."

"I guess we have." He picked up the bag of goodies and Aidyn picked up the pie and they walked toward the door. She'd have to stop watching him walk away. One day. Not today, though. She earned this nice little show.

Just as she was staring at his backside, before she could register what was happening, she was looking at his front. Her eyes snapped up to see his eyes watching her. He chuckled, then winked at her before stepping out the door.

He. Winked. At. Her.

Her breathing came in spurts, and she took in several deep breaths. Watching out the window until his truck pulled away from the parking lot, she finally felt as though her legs would carry her to the door. She twisted the lock and tugged on the chain to the open sign and began straightening chairs around the tables. Then she picked up the empty trays from her glass case and carried them to the kitchen to start baking for tomorrow.

Today, her major sales came from cookies and breads. So, she'd make half again what she'd made for today and see if that would carry her through.

A knock on her back door halted her movements, and her heart rate sped up. She listened for another knock or any sound and silently chastised herself for not wearing her weapon as she'd told her father she would do.

Another knock sounded, this time louder, and she tiptoed to the back door. The BRR wouldn't knock. She felt stupid thinking they would.

Her phone vibrated, and she pulled it from her pocket to see a text from Shianne.

"I'm at your back door."

She quickly twisted the locks and pulled the door open. The instant she saw Shianne's face, she gasped.

"God, I was scared."

"I told you it was me."

"I know, but I guess my mind was stuck on it being someone tricking me."

She grabbed Shianne and hugged her tightly to her.

Shianne whispered. "It's okay Lara. I don't blame you for being scared. It'll take some time."

She pulled back and huffed out a big breath. "Whew. I guess fear, added to exhaustion, made me overreact. I'm sorry."

Shianne laughed and pulled her into the kitchen. She halted, twisted the lock in the door, then continued into the bakery to show her friend the empty cases.

"Look at this."

"Oh, my God. You sold everything? As in, ev-er-y-thing?"

"Yep. The last of the items walked out the door just before you got here. Tate and his friend Aidyn came in and bought what I had left."

"Tate?" She clucked her tongue. "I'm thinking there might be something going on here with Tate."

"Nothing. But he is sexy, and it certainly isn't a hard-ship to see him."

"I've been hearing the girls in town tittering on about these guys. I guess the two women who work with them are knockouts, too! Just what we need is competition."

Lara laughed, then stepped back into the kitchen. "Tate caught me watching his ass."

"No way! Tell me all about it."

ELEVEN

Taro pulled into the parking lot of Lara's Delights and shut his truck off. Her lights weren't on yet, and honestly, he probably shouldn't make this a habit. But, he had a sweet tooth, and she made the best cookies he'd ever tasted. And the coffee at the construction site sucked. It literally sucked.

So, why not start the day off with things he enjoyed? Spencer and Aidyn had gone to the construction site already; he'd be there a few minutes behind them.

The lights turned on; he hopped from his truck and sauntered to the front door. The aroma that wafted over him the instant he pulled the door open made his mouth water.

"Dang, it smells good in here."

Lara's laugh caused goose bumps to form on his body. When he gazed into her eyes though, he felt his heartbeat speed up so much that he felt it in the hollow of his neck.

"Well, good morning. That's a great way to start my day."

Swallowing, he smiled. "It looks like we'll both be starting our days off great, then."

"Are you looking for cookies this morning?"

"I'd like nothing more."

She giggled. "Okay then. Today I felt a bit more creative and decorated some construction cookies."

She pointed to the case, and he chuckled. "Those look amazing."

She beamed, and he couldn't stop staring at her smile. The bell from the door sounded, and he turned to see Spencer and Aidyn enter the bakery.

"Dang, it smells great in here." Spencer boasted.

Aidyn chuckled and glanced his way. The grin on his face was vexing and the hairs on his neck stood and prickled.

Spencer sauntered to the counter next to him. "You look fresh as a daisy this morning, Lara."

Her cheeks turned pink and Tate swallowed. If Spencer had designs on Lara, he'd back away. They had to live together, and he was the team leader, he'd do nothing that would cause trouble.

Lara responded softly. "Thank you."

Her eyes darted between the two of them, and Tate took a deep breath. "I'll take the construction cookies and a coffee, please."

"All of them?"

"Yes. I'll share them with everyone at the site. Including these two knuckleheads."

Aidyn chuckled, and Spencer nodded. "Sounds great. I'll take a coffee too." Spencer turned his head to Aidyn. "Aid, you want coffee?"

"I sure do." That grin still rested on Aidyn's face. That sly smirk unnerved him more than Spencer's interest in

Lara did. Though that did him in a bit, too. His heart felt heavy and his day just grew gloomier.

Lara pulled the cookies from the glass case and arranged them in a box, then poured the three coffees. She set them on the counter and pointed to the end. "Creamer and sugar are down there."

Tate mentally calculated the cost, laid thirty dollars on the counter and picked up his coffee and the cookies. "I'll see you guys out there. Have a great day, Lara."

Before she could say anything, he sauntered out the door without looking back. He'd get creamer at the construction office and go about his day. He huffed out a big breath as he drove into the lot at the construction site and muttered, "Don't be a baby about this."

Carrying his box of cookies into the office at the site, he set them on the table next to the coffee. Baxter boomed, "What do you have in there?"

He plastered on a grin and looked at the older man. "Cookies. And they're decorated like construction equipment."

"Well, that I've got to see." Baxter made his way over to the box of cookies as Tate added creamer to his coffee and reattached the lid to his cup.

"Well, I'll be damned. You got those at Lara's, didn't you? She makes the prettiest cookies in town. My wife buys her cookies all the time."

"I did." He pulled one that looked like a bulldozer from the box. "Help yourself. I'm in a sharing mood today."

"Well, thank you Tate. I appreciate it."

Tate turned to leave. "Spencer and Aidyn are pulling in now. We'll get started on the security cameras right away. Any issues last night?"

"Not that anyone's discovered. Thank God."

"Good to know." He exited the trailer, munching on his cookie, and met Aidyn and Spencer at the tailgate of Spencer's truck.

"No issues last night."

Aidyn picked up a yellow construction tote and set it on the ground. "That's good. We should be able to set up the entire system today with the three of us working on it."

Spencer hefted another construction tote from the truck. "Tate, think Baxter will let us use one of his UTVs? It would be easier to get through some of the narrow areas than with a truck."

"Great idea. I'll go have a chat about that."

"Bring me a cookie on your way out."

Tate halted for a split second, then glanced at Aidyn. "You want one too?"

"I do for sure."

Nodding, he meandered to the trailer and up the steps. Baxter chuckled when he walked in. "Damn, these are good. I just sent a picture of the cookies to my wife. I'd never seen construction cookies."

Tate chuckled. "Mind if we use one of the UTVs?"

"Not at all. Take what you want. Keys are in them all."

"You leave the keys in them?"

Baxter grinned. "What do I look like? Hell no. I pull them out and bring them home with me every night. First thing I do when I get out of my truck in the morning is put them all back in so the guys can use them."

Tate's cheeks heated. "Good move." But he felt stupid questioning Baxter on that. No one had more to lose than he did.

He grabbed two cookies and exited. Handing Aidyn

and Spencer each their cookie, he nodded to the UTVs. "We can take any of them we want. Do you have a preference? I'll go get it."

Spencer bit into his cookie. "Nah. Whichever one you grab will work."

Tate ambled over to the UTVs and decided he liked the black and red one the best. At least he'd get to have a bit of fun driving the UTVs around today. It took a bit of the sting out of the morning.

TWELVE

She felt disappointed when Tate left this morning. Something had happened when Spencer and Aidyn walked in. His jaw tightened, and he left as soon as he could. He also laid money on the counter, and she was concerned about the payment of the security system. It had to be expensive. It was super nice, and she loved sitting on her phone at home and looking at the cameras to make sure everything was fine.

The morning was busy, not as much as the day before, but busier than the norm, and many of the townsfolk offered their commiseration for her troubles and happiness that she was back up and running again.

She had a brief break in the action at eleven and ran back to the kitchen to put a tray of cookies in the oven and knead her bread dough for baking tomorrow morning. She'd knead it once more before she left and it would rise overnight. It made the bakery smell so good.

Shianne stopped in a few minutes later. "Hey. I brought you some lunch. The diner has homemade potato soup today. I know how much you love it."

"Thank you."

Shianne set the container of soup on the corner of her baking table and pulled spoons from the drawer. She opened the refrigerator and found a soda.

"Are we eating in here or out there?"

"Why don't we eat out there today?"

"Sure thing." Shianne picked up their soups, spoons, and napkins and Lara grabbed their sodas.

Shianne picked the lime green table in the middle of the large window. It was her favorite table. Likely because she'd painted it, but it also sat in the middle of the window and they had a view of the road both ways, so she didn't mind it at all.

"So, don't be mad at me, but I saved a dress for you today."

"Shianne... I don't..."

"Shh. You have to join me. You can be my date. Unless you've decided you'll go with Tate with the fine ass."

She laughed. "Oh, my God. You are something." She sipped in a spoonful of soup. "He hasn't asked, and actually, this morning he went all cold on me. I don't know what happened there, but it was weird today."

Shianne tossed her dark blonde hair over her shoulder. "Men! They're so fickle."

She laughed, and it felt good. The dark weight that had fallen this morning lifted.

"You're funny Shi. Thank you. I needed to laugh about it."

"Okay, so after work, I'll bring your dress by, and you can try it on. It's perfect for you. It's blue, the same color as your eyes, and it fades to white at the bottom and it's covered with gold applique. It's perfect. You'll look stunning in it. It flows like a princess gown."

"Shi...I've had a ton of expenses and no insurance checks yet. I simply don't..."

"Stop it. I'll sell it at cost, and I don't have to send the money to the supplier for thirty days. It's all good and you'll absolutely knock Tate off his feet with it."

"I didn't say I was going with him. I said he acted weird today. And..."

"They'll have to go if they want to meet the towns-folk. The one place everyone will be is the ball. Maybe one of those other guys would be my date. That way, we don't have to go alone like we can't find dates. And, we'll be the envy of all the younger ladies in town because we got to spend time with the new guys."

Lara laughed at her friend. "You're too much."

Shianne smiled at her. "I knew I could get you to laugh. I'll bring the dress by tonight after work and you can at least look at it."

"I'll look. You've got my curiosity piqued now, anyway. I have to see this amazing dress."

"Gawd. You'll be the envy of the whole town."

"I doubt that."

A car pulled into the parking lot, and Lara stood. "Sorry, I have to go back to work. Thank you for thinking of me." She leaned down and kissed Shianne's temple, then made her way behind the counter and washed her hands.

An older lady and a little boy entered the bakery, and the little guy ran right to the glass case and ogled the baked goods.

"Hello. How can I help you?"

"Hi, dear. I live in Brookswood and heard about your delicious banana bread and cookies. I'm having my bridge club tonight and I'd love to wow the ladies with your goodies."

"That's wonderful. Thank you. I have cookies here." She pointed to the cookies in the case. "And if you see nothing you want here, I can decorate some for you. It'll take me about an hour to get them decorated and let them set up, but it can be done."

"Oh, that sounds perfect."

Shianne stood and scooped up their empty lunch containers, wiped the table with a napkin and waved as she walked out the front door. Lara's heart felt lighter as she helped her customer.

At four o'clock on the dot, Shianne walked in the front door with a dress bag.

"You had to close up early to be here right at four."

Shianne shrugged. "There wasn't anyone around and I'm excited for you to see this beauty."

She hung the dress on the utility room door, which was just to the left of the bakery counter. She unzipped the bag and gently removed the bag from the shoulders of the dress. Lara stood transfixed as Shianne revealed the dress to her.

She stepped forward and touched the pretty netting and the gold applique. The strapless top showcased an interesting, pleated front. The blue was unusual, just like her eyes, and the transition from blue to white created a stunning visual.

"Wow."

"Right? I knew you'd love it. As soon as I saw it, I knew you needed to have it."

Shianne clapped her hands together. "Oh, wait." She picked the hanger off the door and spun the dress around. "Look. The back laces up."

"Wow. It's stunning."

"I know! I know! Hold it up to you."

Lara's fingers shook as she took the hanger in her hands and pulled the dress tightly to her. She looked down at it and the way it fanned out made her feel like she'd glide across the floor.

The doorbell rang, and she looked up to see Tate and Spencer standing before her.

His eyes blazed into hers, and it felt like the world had stopped moving for a moment.

Shianne started talking. "I'll bet you're Tate." His eyes then moved to Shianne's. "And you must be Spencer. Lara told me she'd met you guys."

Tate turned his million-watt smile on Shi as he introduced himself. "Yes. Tate Vickers." She giggled as he shook her hand.

Spencer repeated the action. "Spencer Lawson. Nice to meet you."

"So, this is the dress I picked out for Lara for the Bourbon Ball. Isn't it fantastic?"

Tate nodded. "It is. It matches your eyes."

He said it softly, but she heard it. Her heart squeezed tightly, and her body heated. She felt the prickling in her chest, and she knew she was bright red.

Shianne clapped her hands. "I know. You guys need to meet people in town. You should come to the Bourbon Ball. It so happens, we don't have dates."

She looked at Shianne and shook her head. That girl. But the cat was out of the bag now. She locked eyes with Tate.

"Tate, would you be my date for the Bourbon Ball? Spencer and Shianne can go together, and if you need us to find dates for your friends, we'll see what we can do."

Spencer chuckled. "That sounds fun. And it appears this ball is formal?"

Shianne responded, "It is. But I can get you hooked up with a tux if you need me to. I have a friend in Brookswood who owns a larger shop than mine and they carry tux rentals, too."

"When is this Bourbon Ball?" Spencer asked.

"It's in two weeks. It's THE event of the year around here."

Shianne and Spencer chatted, but she stopped listening when Tate stepped forward and asked softly. "Is this what you want? Me as your date, not Spencer?"

"Yes. Why would you think otherwise?"

His cheeks heated and the soft smile that graced his lips seemed as though he was surprised and, she hoped, happy. Then it dawned on her that this morning, Spencer had complimented her, and Tate must have thought she was interested in Spencer.

She thought only women jumped to conclusions.

THIRTEEN

Tate's phone rang, and he reached for it from a deep sleep. "Vickers."

"Tate, it's Baxter. Those fuckers are out at the site, damaging the pipe we just installed."

"We're on it. Call the sheriff."

He sprung from his bed and ran out to the hall. Rapping on Spencer's door, then Henry's, then Aidyn's, he yelled. "Gotta go." He continued down the hall to Maya and Adelaide's rooms. "Trouble at the construction site."

His teammates all sprang from their beds, and he ran back to his room to dress. Within ten minutes, they had loaded into two vehicles and headed to the construction site. He drove his truck and Henry drove his. Aidyn was in the back seat of his truck, checking ammo on weapons and making sure they were ready.

He heard the sirens blaring and arrived at the construction site just after the sheriff. In the distance, vehicles revved their engines. He rolled his window down and listened to them tear up the road.

He stopped alongside the sheriff's vehicle, and they exited as the sheriff shined his light on the pipe where there was some slight damage, but nothing appeared beyond repair.

Baxter turned to him. "They didn't damage as much as they wanted. I think we're going to have to go up the mountain tomorrow and talk to Everett Howard. We can't have this. I'll need a couple of you to go with me."

Tate nodded. "I'll go with you." Aidyn responded next. "I'll go too."

Maya stepped forward. "I'll stay here the rest of the night in case they come back."

Henry agreed. "That's a good idea. I'll stay with you."

Tate looked around at the fencing, seeing the damaged links and holes cut into it. "So the fencing doesn't keep them out. Might have to construct a concrete wall around the base."

"Believe me, I've thought of it. Getting anyone from the government to agree to that is like pulling teeth. They just keep telling us to handle the people of our town. They don't listen to the fact that they aren't from our town, and we have little control over them."

Tate turned to the sheriff. "What happened at your meeting with the town council the other night?"

The Sheriff scratched his forehead. "The council is in a spot. They've declined the tax deferment due to a lot of pressure from the mayor and believe the BRR won't come up with the money to pay the taxes. I simply don't understand why they think the BRR will just move on. It isn't going to happen and no matter how much I try to explain it, they don't want to hear it." The sheriff rubbed the back of his head. "At the same time, the council doesn't want to start a war. That's exactly what they're doing by not approving the tax deferment. We have some younger members on the council right now and many of them weren't around during the previous war. And memories fade."

Aidyn shook his head. "So, basically, the council is taking the coward's way out by not doing anything but expecting money to be forthcoming. What happens when the BRR brings the war down the mountain?"

The sheriff looked at him and Tate actually felt sorry for the man. He was caught in the middle with little authority to do anything. "I don't know Aidyn. I just don't know."

Aidyn glanced at him, and his jaw tightened. He shook his head, then turned around and surveyed the area.

Henry and Maya walked the perimeter of the area where the BRR was messing around, and Tate looked at his crew. "As soon as Henry and Maya feel the area is secured, we'll head home."

Baxter looked around, then his eyes landed on Tate. "Your cameras helped us out this time."

"It appears so. From this point forward, we'll also be on site twenty-four-seven. Henry and Maya will stay the rest of tonight. We'll go back to a regular schedule tomorrow. We'd thought the cameras would be enough, but we'll need to be more diligent."

"Thank you for that. I appreciate it."

Henry and Maya came back from their perimeter check. Henry nodded. "It's all good. We'll be around all night. If we can get the keys to the office, we can stay in there, monitor the cameras from inside, and we can look around every hour if we feel something's amiss."

Baxter pulled the keys from his pocket and pulled the

office key from his key ring. "I'll get new ones made tomorrow for each of you."

They loaded up and said good night, then drove home. Tate looked at Spencer, "We should have a camera feed here at the house, too. That way, we'll be aware before Baxter."

Spencer shrugged. "Baxter said he didn't think that was necessary."

"I know, but I think it is. And, since it's our asses on the line if the base isn't built on time, we'll do what we think is necessary from this point on."

Aidyn gripped his shoulder and shook him. "There you go. I think we need to take care of those little shits from the BRR too. We're outsiders, so it isn't like the sheriff or any of the townsfolk are going up there. It'll be us. Outsiders. Maybe we can make them see the light."

"It doesn't appear they fear much, but I think you're right. It's time we take over some of this shit. These folks here fear another war. And those bastards up there know it."

Adelaide chuckled. "Yep, they know it all right. They shot at an officer a couple of days ago and nothing happened."

"That's the truth, Addy." Tate took a deep breath. "I'm going to get some shut-eye. I'll head to the site early in the morning, around four, and relieve Maya and Henry. They didn't have a full night's sleep and I'll take a bit of the load off them."

Aidyn waved as he walked up the stairs. "I'll go with you."

Tate flopped on his bed and stared up at the ceiling. Even with all of this going through his mind, what he saw was the image of Lara holding that dress in front of her.

He couldn't wait to see her in it. And he was relieved that Spencer wasn't mad at all. He seemed excited to go to the ball with Shianne, and that relieved him more than he cared to admit. Now, if they could just figure out how to teach those BRR bastards to stay up there where they belonged, life would be perfect.

FOURTEEN

Lara swallowed and let out a slow breath to calm the butterflies in her tummy as Sharon Jackson, her mom's best friend, told her of the trouble in town last night.

"They robbed the gas station and beat up Flynn DeMario. He's not in the hospital anymore. He went in for stitches and was released. Then, they went on over to Paxton's and broke the windows and smashed the glass cases here. Mr. Paxton hid in the back, but not before he fell and broke his ankle running from them. That poor man hid in the freezer for an hour."

"Oh, my God. I'm so sorry to hear all of this. It's just getting worse and worse."

"It certainly is, Lara. I sure hope your place doesn't get hit again."

She inhaled a deep breath and closed her eyes. "Me too, Sharon. Me too."

"Anyway, I hear there are some new boys in town and from what I heard over at Homemade in the Hollow, they're lookers."

She laughed nervously. "They are lookers."

"Oh, you've seen them?"

"I have."

"Do you think they'll come to the Bourbon Ball? It would bring in a lot more people if they were. Folks can't wait to get a look at them."

Lara's cheeks grew warm, and she swallowed the lump in her throat. "I heard a couple of them were coming for sure."

"Good! I can't wait to see what all the fuss is about."

Lara nodded, not wanting to say more. Luckily Sharon had chatted herself out and couldn't wait to go on to the next stop and tell all she knew. She picked up her bakery bag, filled with blueberry muffins, and waved as she headed to the door. "Stay safe now, Lara. I'll stop by and visit your mama in a little while."

"Sounds good. I know she loves your visits."

As the door closed behind Sharon, she let out a big huff of air and headed back to the kitchen to bring out fresh muffins that had been cooling on the table.

Sirens sounded, and she looked out the front window only to see the Jeep that had been here when those jerks wrecked her place. She felt her side and realized she'd once again not put her weapon on this morning and chastised herself for not being prepared. She needed to carry again until they caught those kids.

Her fingers shook, but she locked her door and pulled the string on the light until the sirens stopped and hopefully those BRR kids were headed back up the mountain.

Her knees shook; she pulled out a chair and watched out the window from her seat. Tugging her phone out of her back pocket, she dialed Shianne.

"Hey, I see they're back down here again."

"Yeah. I locked my door. But I'm shaking like a leaf, Shi."

"I know you are, honey. I'll stay on the phone with you. I've locked my door too."

"Okay. I just hate this."

"Me too."

The Jeep came roaring into her parking lot, and Lara screamed. "He's here. Oh my God, he's here."

"You get in the back, Lara. You hear me?"

Lara stood and tried to make her legs work, but they felt like lead. Once she'd made it to the kitchen door, she heard him revving his engine out front and tires squealed on the blacktop. She dropped behind the counter to hide. It went on and on. Through the glass of the display case she watched as that same kid, the one with the dark hair, spun cheerios in her parking lot.

"He's just making a mess of the parking lot. He's spinning cheerios."

"Don't let him see you, Lara. He might have his gun."

Her breathing grew thin, and she felt like she couldn't get air. The sirens grew loud again, and Lara saw her father's squad car coming up the road, which caused the kid in the Jeep to peel out of her parking lot and up the road, passing her father's squad car, who spun around in her parking lot and sped off after the BRR kid.

"Lara, honey, what's happening?"

She forgot Shianne was on the phone. "Oh. My dad came down the road and the guy in the Jeep sped off. Dad turned around in the parking lot and took off after him."

"Thank God he isn't there anymore."

"Yeah. Shit, that was scary."

"I know. How about we go do some target practice after work tonight?"

"Yes. That sounds like a great idea. I need to practice and start carrying again."

"Me too."

Tate's truck pulled into the lot and her heart raced for a different reason. "Hey, I have to open the door for Tate."

Shianne chuckled on the other end of the phone, but she didn't wait to listen to her teasing.

She watched as Tate stepped from his vehicle and looked at the burnt rubber in the parking lot. He turned his gaze toward her at the door. His jaw was tight, and his eyes looked hardened.

"Are you hurt?"

He strode toward her, and she stepped back to let him in the bakery.

"No. Just scared."

He stepped close and pulled her to his body, and her arms instantly wrapped around his waist. His arms engulfed her and she felt safe and warm. She closed her eyes and inhaled his fresh masculine scent.

"I'm here now. You're okay."

His words soothed her; his firm body felt like armor wrapped around her and she relaxed as he held her.

After a few minutes, he pulled back, and she tilted her head up to look at him. It was electric when his lips molded to hers. His whiskers brushed her face, and she savored the roughness of it. She opened her mouth, and his tongue touched her lips then slid inside. Their tongues danced with each other, and her heart skipped when she tasted her cookies on him.

The sounds of approaching sirens had them pulling

apart, but he stared into her eyes for a long time. He touched his lips with his fingers as if he'd never felt a kiss before. Then he licked his lips before stepping back.

A car door slammed. Her father entered the bakery and broke the spell that had fallen over them.

FIFTEEN

Tate drove to the base at the butt crack of dawn like he'd promised, but he missed his coffee and cookies. And Lara. He missed seeing her smile first thing in the morning.

Aidyn sat in the passenger seat, yawning and stretching. "I should have taken the night shift."

Tate laughed. "I was thinking the same thing. I think it's easier staying up than it is getting up."

"So, I asked my dad and mom to pull up the treaty the BRR has with the town of Glen Hollow. I actually think it might be with the state of Kentucky, but I want to know that. Then, if it's what I think it is, we can take action accordingly."

"Such as?"

"I suspect the treaty is with the state of Kentucky. But I think it might be a federal treaty at its core, with the state signing as a third party."

"You're thinking Casper can offer some leverage?"

"I'm not sure. I'd think he would have given us that in the beginning if that was the case. But once I read the treaty, we'll see if we can wrangle some options to keep those guys up on the mountain."

Aidyn laughed and straightened his legs.

Tate turned into the site parking area and shut off his truck. Henry and Maya exited the trailer and waved as they descended the stairs.

"Any issues during the night?"

Maya shook her head. Her ponytail was slightly askew, but otherwise she still looked raring to go. "No. We heard the vehicles ripping up and down the hill last night. I don't know if they were trying to intimidate us or what their deal was, but they didn't come down all the way. At least not over here."

"That's good." Tate said.

Henry brushed his hands down his face. "Yeah, I found how they've been getting in here, though. Maybe you can have the fence fixed at the rear of the property. They cut the fencing, then bent the wire and hooked it back, just like the hooks on the back of a woman's dress. It won't stop them from cutting it again, but Spencer can set up a camera back there and we can stop them before they get too far with it."

Tate nodded. "Interesting analogy."

Henry's middle finger popped up.

Tate laughed. "Okay, great. And we're all going to the Bourbon Ball in two weeks. So, we'll need to get tuxes and Maya and Adelaide will need dresses. I understand there's a boutique in town called Divine Designs. It's owned by Shianne Brown and she's been dressing all the women in town for the ball. You two should make a trip in there today or tomorrow."

Maya's nose wrinkled, and she shrugged. "I could wear a tux."

"You can do that if you prefer. I'm not your clothing police. Just find something to wear and plan on attending the ball. It's a good time for us to meet the townsfolk and get to know who's who."

Henry puffed his cheeks and let out a long breath, then he and Maya walked toward his truck to leave. Henry called over his shoulder, "Fresh coffee is in the pot. You can thank Maya."

He chuckled. "Thanks, Maya."

Tate followed Aidyn up the metal steps to the construction office and headed to the coffeepot for his first cup of coffee this morning. As he poured, his stomach tightened slightly. It didn't smell like Lara's coffee, and he already knew it wouldn't taste like it either. That first sip reminded him he was right.

Aidyn chuckled, "It's not Lara's, is it?"

"That's a fact."

Pulling his laptop from its case, he set it up on the desk and pulled up the security cameras. His phone rang, and he saw his dad's photo on the screen.

"Hey, Dad."

"Hey, Tate. I just emailed you the treaty. Your thoughts are right on and this should help a lot with gaining leverage there."

"Thanks, Dad. Hope you weren't up all night."

"No, your mom emailed Casper, and it was here when I woke this morning."

Tate chuckled. "Tell Mom thank you. I'll call her later and tell her myself."

"How are you settling in?"

"Pretty good. We've had a few issues with the BRR, but we're not sitting back and watching. We have access to the treaty now and we'll use it against them."

"That's my boy."

"Talk to you later, Dad. Aidyn and I just got to the construction site, and I want to read through everything."

"You got it, Tate. Love you."

"Love you too, Dad."

Aidyn sat next to him at the front of the desk and opened his laptop, simultaneously taking a large drink of the bitter coffee.

"Ugh. That's harsh."

Tate laughed. He clicked on the email from his dad, then opened the attachment and began reading the treaty.

As he read through it, the verbiage he'd hoped to find was there. Usually a treaty was between different nations, but in the preamble it stated that the BRR insisted it be called a treaty, as if they were their own nation.

There were consequences for breaking a treaty and the consequences listed in this matter were:

"…the treaty is hereby broken upon the death of one party at the hands of the other party. The consequences of death at the hands of the opposing party are the end of the treaty and the BRR will become US citizens and will uphold the laws of the US government and will abide by said laws. Forcible removal from the lands…"

Tate continued reading, then sat forward, "Aidyn, here it is."

"Repeated offenses of vandalism, fear mongering, and threats of violence, up to or including death, will irrevocably break this treaty." He continued reading the definition, "in this case, it means consecutive thirty days of the offending action."

"They'll stop before their thirty days are up. And as far as we're aware, they have killed no one. But the damage to businesses has been ongoing now for ten days. Plus, I think we can convince the president that shooting at a police officer and hitting the vehicle of a citizen is a threat to the deputy, you, Adelaide, Spencer, and myself as we were behind the squad car and in danger."

Aidyn nodded, "Let's use it. What do we have to lose?"

Two hours later, Spencer and Adelaide pulled into the parking lot, looking ready to tackle the day.

Spencer opened the construction office door first, "I just saw Baxter out by the basement of the main building. He said you're going up to the BRR today?"

Tate stood and stretched. "Yes, Aidyn and me. We're going to see if we can work on a better truce."

Spencer nodded. "I like it. Do you need backup?"

"Not this time. Just keep your phones on in case we need help and watch for any exacerbated activity while we're up there. They may take our interference as a sign of aggression and start acting up again."

"Will do."

Adelaide set her laptop on the table and logged in.

Tate and Aidyn left the construction trailer and headed for his truck. As he pulled from the construction lot, he passed the first road up the mountain.

Aidyn glanced over. "You don't want Baxter to know we're going up?"

"No. He's too mad right now at the delays and I think we need to remain cool. At least this time."

Aidyn laughed and put his head on the headrest behind him.

Tate turned up the next road leading to what he hoped was Everett Howard and a resolution to the unrest with the BRR.

He saw something glimmer in the sunlight ahead and slowed down as they neared. Within seconds, two four-wheelers popped up onto the road from the brush. The two men hopped off their vehicles and stood between their four-wheelers and Tate's truck. Their arms were crossed over their chests and their jaws were locked in confidence.

He stopped his truck and said to Aidyn. "Well, here goes."

"Yep." Aidyn opened his door and stepped out first, Tate followed suit. They strode to the front of his truck.

"I'm Tate Vickers and this is my teammate, Aidyn Dunbar. We're here to see Everett Howard."

The first man, the larger of the two looked at his partner, nodded, then jerked his head toward the top of the mountain.

With a scowl on his face the second man jumped on his four-wheeler and took off up the mountain. He spun his tires enough to pelt Aidyn and him with stones and he heard a few taps as they hit his truck. Since he'd been here, his truck had fared worse than everything else.

Tate tried engaging in conversation. "What's your name?"

"What's it to ya? Gonna ask me out on a date?"

"Just trying to be friendly."

"We're not friends. Ain't gonna be neither."

"Point taken."

He glanced at Aidyn, who shrugged and leaned against the front of his truck. He stared at the other man and Tate took the chance to look around.

From this vantage point, the trees were still full and the brush was wild and unkept. It provided cover for their four-wheelers as they hid, and he guessed they kept it that way for just that reason.

The sound of a motor growing closer made him look behind the man standing before him for the second man to approach.

The dust from the road rose up and the second man appeared soon after. When he stopped his four-wheeler, he spun slightly toward them, once again pelting them with stones and dust. It was getting irritating.

"Everett says he'll see you."

Tate nodded and turned to get into his truck. "Nope. You're on foot from here."

"No, we're not going up there on foot without any protection."

The two men looked at each other and laughed. But the first man shrugged his shoulder. "Suit yourself."

He and Aidyn climbed into his truck and followed the two men on four-wheelers. It didn't take him long to realize why they thought it was funny he wanted to bring his truck up the mountain. The terrain quickly turned to narrow rutted-out dirt paths. The overgrown brush scraped the side of his truck and, once again, he thought about his poor truck. He'd worked long and hard to afford this vehicle and it kept taking the brunt of this mission.

They bounced around for a while before finally Aidyn sat up straight and said, "Stop." He shook his head. "Let's walk. They're doing this on purpose. We'll walk up there, we have weapons if we need them and when we come back down, we'll hop in here and take our time coming down without completely destroying your truck."

He put the truck in park and pulled the keys. "Agreed."

They exited the truck and began walking up the hill.

The two men who were leading stopped up ahead and laughed and he tightened his jaw in irritation.

By the time the terrain had leveled he had sweat dripping down his back, and his legs were twitching from the workout. Note to self—add hill climbing to my exercise routine.

The overgrown brush thinned and the grade leveled off. The two men parked their four-wheelers and waited there for him and Aidyn.

Aidyn mumbled, "Fuckers."

"Yeah."

As they drew close, he saw their camp. Or town, or whatever they called it. Homemade cabins were built around a central area. In the middle of the central area was a large fire pit. The cabins were not of equal size or distance but placed where they were on level ground. Some were more neatly made than others. Some with superior craftsmanship, while others looked like something tossed together to get through a night. Since money wasn't something that the BRR exchanged with each other, it was interesting to see even up here there were classes.

"Hurry up. Everett is waiting."

He shook his head and moved along behind the two men, Aidyn alongside him.

They sauntered between two nice-sized cabins and to an area that was sheltered and located at the foot of another large hill. It provided shelter for the cabin nestled at the base of it on two sides. The trees provided shade from the heat and the temperature felt a few degrees cooler in this area.

The two men stepped up on the large front porch and knocked. The door opened and a man stepped from inside looking like an old-world Santa. He had long white hair which he left hanging free. It blended with a long white beard. His clothing was simple, but also interesting. He wore pants in a khaki color, but they were homemade and had few pockets or visible stitching on the straight legs. The shirt he wore was loose fitting and hung over the top of the pants. The style reminded him of hospital scrubs. But over all of that, he wore a long vest-type garment that hung to the ground and swirled around like a cape. It was trimmed in what looked like squirrel tails and fur of some sort.

He stood tall and imposing, and he didn't say a word. Tate decided to do the same. He and Aidyn stood tall and proud, shoulders back, and waited for this man, whom he presumed was Everett Howard, to speak.

"Why are you here to see me?"

"I'd like to talk to you about the treaty and the things that have been going on in Glen Hollow."

"What do you know about any of it?"

"I've read the treaty and my truck is now sporting two nice bullet holes thanks to one of your men."

"And you want me to stop sending my men down the mountain and making the townspeople pay for the injustice they have just handed us?"

"What injustice?"

"The tax deferment has been ongoing for sixty years. At the time, my father was assured it would stand forever as long as we stayed up here and didn't cause trouble."

"It appears you didn't stay up here."

"We did until the trade stopped."

"So, the trade stopped and that's what prompted all of this?"

He didn't move. He stood on his porch passing judgment. At least that's what it felt like.

Aidyn spoke for the first time. "Some of the businesses are still trading with you."

"Not enough of them. And that's because of the mayor."

Tate inhaled. "The free enterprise system works this way: you have something of value to offer, someone will pay for it. If you don't, they won't. Since you're now stealing products to manufacture your elixir, they don't feel as though they should have to pay for it, since they supplied some of the product. You have a lopsided system here and the townspeople are tired of it."

"What do you know of any of it?"

"I just told you, I've been down there. I've spoken to the townspeople, and I know their complaints."

"You know only of Lara's complaints."

Shock was a light word for Lara's name coming out of Everett's mouth. Also, the realization that Everett knew he had spoken to Lara told him they were watching very closely. He stood stock-still though and didn't let on that any of this bothered him.

"I know of many business owners' complaints."

Everett shrugged. "I don't care. Once in a while our youngsters misbehave. It's no different than the townie boys doing the same up here. They sneak up the mountain and try sampling our elixir without paying. They hunt on our lands. They've also tried sampling our women from time to time. Why don't you ask Keaton about that?"

Tate stared into his blue eyes. Creases around his light blue eyes told the story of hardship, years in the sun, and toil. Even though their population up here didn't match the population below, it was nevertheless difficult keeping a group of people in line. To follow whatever laws they used up here. Clearly, they didn't care for the fraternizing between the BRR and townspeople.

Tate nodded slightly. "I'd like to go back down with an agreement. Even a small one to begin with."

"What agreement do you have in mind?"

"Tell your people to stop coming down the hill and robbing and damaging businesses. They've done quite a bit of damage the past month. It needs to stop."

"And what will you do for us?"

"If I have your agreement, I'll talk to the mayor about letting the deferment go through."

"I want the deferment to be a forever event. I shouldn't have to pay taxes on land that I own rightfully. I'm not using your services, for which the taxes are paid. We don't use your police and fire services. We don't use your schools. We shouldn't have to pay taxes. Ever."

"I can't guarantee that Everett. I'll pass it along and see if I can. But, in the meantime, please keep your men up here as an act of good faith."

Everett glared at him. He then glared at Aidyn. It felt like an eternity, but he wasn't going to break the eye contact or flinch.

"You tell that mayor to defer our taxes forever. If you can get that done, we'll leave the townsfolk alone."

"That includes Fort Abraham?"

"Fuck. No!" Everett paced across his porch, then stopped directly in front of them once more. "That base is on our land. If they want to build there, they'd better pay me taxes!"

"You'll need to show proof that you own that land.

The government has the deed to the land and your name isn't on it."

Everett stared. He spat on the ground, directly in front of Tate's shoe. Tate tightened his jaw as he stared at the older man.

Everett turned. "You have my orders."

He stepped into his cabin, and they were roundly dismissed.

The two men who escorted them up the hill moved to either side of them and nodded toward the road down the mountain. "Let's go."

SIXTEEN

Lara stretched and prepared for another busy day at the bakery. Just before she left last night, the Bourbon Ball Committee Chair, Millie LeBeau, called and ordered twelve dozen cookies for the ball. She'd get a start on the cookies and freeze them until she had the time to decorate them next weekend. After showering and dressing, the lights in her house clicked off. She tried several switches; none of them worked.

She pressed her back to the wall of her bedroom and listened to any noise in the house. Her heart thumped so hard she felt her body move with each beat. Her breathing grew shallow, and her knees shook. Were they here? In her house?

After a few moments of quiet, she swallowed and slowly peeled herself from the wall. Sliding her feet lightly across the floor she listened intently for any movement or sound. Sliding the drawer on her night stand open, she removed her holster and buckled it on, then her pistol from inside and slid it into the holster. Feeling inside the drawer for her extra magazine, she gripped it tightly and pushed it into the loop on her holster. Taking a deep breath, she stepped from the relative safety of her bedroom and into the short hallway that led to her kitchen and living room. She had a second bathroom across the hall from the spare bedroom.

Gripping the phone tightly in her hand, she tapped the flashlight icon and lit the area in front of her. She scanned the kitchen as she entered the room. Nothing was amiss. No one was inside. Still unnerved, she moved into the living room, grateful she had an empty wall to push herself against.

Moving her flashlight back and forth and she let out a heavy breath when all seemed in place. She rested her head against the wall for a moment and willed her breathing to return to normal and her heartbeat to settle.

She pulled up the security camera on her phone to check the bakery but couldn't get a visual, and the error message on the camera said it was 'offline'. She grabbed her jacket from the hall closet, then stepped into the garage and tapped the opener on the wall before realizing it wasn't going to open.

She glanced at her phone. It was close to three thirty in the morning and she had work to do. Rather than waking her father up, she pulled the ladder from the wall and opened it under the emergency pull to open her garage door manually.

She pulled the red handle and released the door opener from the door, then replaced her ladder. She lifted the door and pushed it open above her head, struggling slightly from the weight of it. She drove her vehicle out of the garage, stopped, closed the door, then jumped back in her vehicle to get to the bakery. If luck was on her side, she'd only be a couple of minutes late. Not that she answered to anyone. But, still.

The sun wouldn't shine for a couple of hours, and the stars still shone in the sky. It was these moments right here that made her love Glen Hollow all over again. But this morning's events so far reminded her there was a dark force running rampant through town these days and she needed to be vigilant.

As she neared the first of only two stoplights in Glen Hollow, she noted it was flashing yellow. That only happened when there'd been a power outage and the returning power had been disrupted.

She looked both ways, then moved ahead, but the little hairs at her nape prickled. She absently brushed the back of her neck with her hand and mentally noted to tell her father what happened here during the night when no one was on duty. Glancing often in her mirror, her shoulders tightened painfully.

As she drove down Main Street, she noted a few of the stores had flashing lights in their store windows and... what was that ahead?

She slowed her vehicle and squinted her eyes. Devine Designs' inside lights blinked furiously in perfect rhythm.

The same thing was happening at Paxton's grocery store and the gas station, and Hairy's Beards, the barbershop in town. In Chestnut Grove, the town's furniture store, and Bloomin Lovely, the flower shop all the lights were flashing too.

She shrugged and called her dad. His phone only rang twice, and he sounded tired when he answered.

"Dad. I'm sorry to wake you, but the power was out in town last night."

The sound of sheets rustling and movement filled her

ears as she waited for her dad to leave the bedroom so he didn't wake her mom. She kept driving to the bakery, but the heavy feeling in her stomach grew each block closer she came to it.

"Okay, honey. Tell me what's going on."

"I'm two blocks from the bakery and every store's lights are flashing. All of them. The stoplights are flashing yellow. The lights were off at my house too."

"Okay honey. I'll get in my squad car and look around. When you get to the bakery, just wait in your car and I'll go in with you to make sure everything is alright in there."

"You don't think the BRR had anything to do with this do you?"

"I don't know what's going on. But if all the lights are flashing, and they're watching, it may be a siren's call for them to come down and cause trouble."

"Oh, God. I'm so sick of this shit."

"I know, honey. We all are. But, until things settle down again, we just need to keep our chins up and ourselves aware."

She inhaled deeply and let out her breath in a whoosh. "Okay. I'll wait for you."

"I'll be there in a few minutes, Lara."

She heard the click as the call ended and continued slowly through town. It was too early to call Shianne and she didn't want to worry her, but her heart beat wildly in her chest, thinking the BRR might be lurking around any corner.

She rotated her head, then stretched her shoulders back as she turned onto Front Street past Porter's Steakhouse to see if the lights were flashing just out of town as well.

As she neared Porter's, Mrs. Porter was outside, pulling something from the raised flowerbed surrounding the building. Lara pulled into the parking lot and got out of her vehicle.

"Good morning Mrs. Porter. Are your lights out here too?"

Mrs. Porter shoved her hands on her hips and her bottom lip quivered. "Yes, they are, and those little BRR bastards threw shit in my flower beds. I saw them do it with my own eyes. I was in the kitchen, adding a rub to our roasts for tonight. When I heard the trucks, I came out to the window and witnessed them throw the trash. I'm so damned sick of them."

"I am too. My dad is on the way to the bakery now to check on things with me before I go inside. I'll ask him to stop here when he's finished. I'd leave that all right there so he can see it."

"Lara, honey, we all love you, but your pa won't do a damned thing to those bastards!"

SEVENTEEN

Tate finished dressing and headed downstairs. Addy had just made coffee and stood in front of the pot, waiting for it to finish brewing.

"You're up early, Addy."

"Yeah. I couldn't sleep. I know I heard that Jeep running up and down the streets last night."

"What time?"

"I guess around two thirty. I kept waiting to hear them come driving our vehicles outside. Our cars and trucks don't have Kentucky plates on them and my guess is, those assholes know what we drive. They're probably driving around looking for our house."

Tate leaned against the counter and crossed his arms in front of his chest. "Yeah. I've been thinking about that. In light of the turmoil here, we'll need to find another place to live. We need to be able to put our vehicles in a garage."

The coffee finished brewing and Addy pulled a couple of mugs from the cupboard. She poured their coffee then sat at the kitchen table. He added his creamer and sat across from her.

"Your wheels are spinning. What are you thinking?"

"There's an old factory out of town. It's not overly big, the company moved out of town and went to Lexington about five years ago. I asked at the diner yesterday and they said they used to make clothing in there. We could take a look at it. Buy it. Convert it. We'd have plenty of room for all of us, plus our vehicles could be hidden inside."

"That's not a bad idea, Addy."

They sipped their coffee in silence until Aidyn clomped down the stairs. "Morning."

"Morning." Addy turned her phone toward him and showed him the factory photographs.

Aidyn sat at the table. "What's that?"

"Addy found an old factory on the edge of town. She's thinking we could turn it into our home base so our vehicles could be inside and we'd have more room."

Addy grinned. "Plus, we'd be doing something good for the community. That should get us brownie points."

Aidyn nodded then scraped his hands through his hair. "Are we going to see the mayor today?"

"Yes. I've already emailed him and asked for a meeting this morning."

Just as the words were out of his mouth, his phone chimed a message. He opened the email app on his phone and found the mayor had responded. "It appears we're on for eight this morning."

"Fantastic."

He grinned at Aidyn. "Did you hear the BRR out and about last night?"

"Yes. Didn't you?"

He shook his head. "No. My bedroom is at the back of the house. I didn't hear anything."

"Lucky fucker."

Tate chuckled and shrugged. "Maybe."

Aidyn stood. "I'm going to shower and get ready. I'll be down in a bit. How about we eat breakfast at the diner this morning?"

"That sounds good."

Aidyn left the room and he nodded toward Addy. "You want to spearhead the factory showing? See when we can get in?"

"Sure can.

"I'll run it past my dad and let him know what we're thinking once we can take a look at it. I know mom looked for a long time to find a place here big enough for all of us and there isn't much available."

"Yeah. Grandma is going to hate to hear that we're thinking of living in a factory."

He laughed. "Poor Pilar. She has sure been put through the wringer between your Aunt Jax, and you and Maya joining GHOST."

"I think she's proud, but she likes giving Aunt Jax grief."

"It's sort of their thing."

Tate walked into the dining room and opened the lid on his laptop. He signed into GHOST's database and wrote his report regarding their discussion with Everett yesterday. Baxter was less than pleased when he heard Everett's comments on the base. They needed to brace for more trouble from the BRR where it was concerned.

He typed in Everett's comments on Keaton and sat back to think about it for a minute. Aidyn stepped into the room and chuckled as he pulled out a chair and sat in it to put his boots on.

"What are you lost in thought over?"

"Everett's comments about Keaton. 'Ask Keaton about the men coming up and sampling our women'."

Aidyn nodded. "I've been wondering about that too."

Tate typed a question in his report, "What does Keaton Bennit know about the men going up the mountain to sample the women?"

Tate took a deep breath and dialed Keaton's number.

"Good morning, Tate. What can I help you with?"

"Good morning. I have a meeting with the mayor at eight o'clock. Is there any time for us to meet beforehand?"

His eyes darted to the clock on his computer and noted it was just after seven.

"Ah..." Keaton huffed out a breath. "I'm at the bakery now. Lara's security system is offline and I asked her to wait until I got here this morning to check things out. Then, I had a few things to do, and I just got back and am having a cup of coffee at the moment. You're welcome to join me here."

"We'll be right there."

He hung up and closed the lid on his laptop. "We're meeting with Keaton at Lara's."

Aidyn chuckled. "Good coffee and cookies. Nice."

Lara heard Tate's truck pull into the lot at the front of her bakery. Looking out the window she saw Aidyn in the passenger seat. She turned over two ceramic coffee cups and filled them. Twisting, she set them on the end of the counter where the creamers and sugar were arranged before pulling two plates from the shelf behind her bakery counter and laid them on top of the bakery case.

Her eyes found her father's and her cheeks heated from his scrutiny. Tate and Aidyn walked in the door, saving her from any conversation with her father about how she knew what they liked, and she smiled.

"Good morning. I have coffee ready for you at the end of the counter and fresh cookies in the case."

Tate's smile transformed his already handsome face into a work of art.

"Good morning and thank you."

Aidyn went directly to the coffee. Tate strode directly to her in front of her bakery case nearest the cookies.

"Those look amazing. I'll take the tree and the house in the front please."

"Thank you." She pulled the cookies from the tray as Tate prepared his coffee.

Aidyn stopped at the glass case and grinned. "Just grab any two for me please."

He pulled money from his wallet and dropped it on the counter. "I've got his too."

Before she could comment he made his way to her father's table near the window.

Tate stopped and picked up the plates with their cookies. "Your security system was out today?"

"Yeah. All the businesses in town had flashing lights and my garage door wouldn't open this morning either."

"We'll take a look at the security system while we're here."

"Thank you."

She watched him juggle the plates of cookies and his coffee. She almost ran around the counter to help him, but with his long legs, it didn't take him more than five steps to reach the table.

She inhaled and busied herself with refilling the bakery case and helping customers. She wanted to know what Tate and Aidyn were speaking to her father about, but she didn't want to appear nosy.

Luckily, or maybe unluckily, she had a steady stream of customers in the bakery as Tate and Aidyn met with her father. She noticed a couple of times how her father's voice raised and she wondered what on earth they were talking about that would make him so angry. She could tell he was uncomfortable by the way he shrugged then rubbed his temples, she had seen him do it hundreds over the years.

She had her cookies cut out and on baking sheets. As soon as she had a break in customer traffic she popped back to the kitchen and slid two pans into the oven. She set her timer and went back to the front of the store as Millie LeBeau entered her store.

"Good morning, Lara. I wanted to stop in and check on your progress with the cookies for the Bourbon Ball."

"I've made several dozen of them. I'll be freezing them until next week then I'll decorate the entire batch. Would you like me to decorate a couple sample cookies for you?"

"Oh, no dear." The sweet lady shook her head and her hands in front of her. "I'm just following up on all of my checklist items."

Tate turned a couple of times and listened to the conversation, or at least it appeared that way.

"Lara, did you hear what the BRR did out at the old sewing factory last night?"

That seemed to grab Tate's attention completely, as he actually turned in his chair and actively listened.

"No. I didn't hear anything."

"Oh, it's just more of the same, I suppose. But they threw rocks at the windows and broke the glass out of them. I just came from there and it is a mess."

"Oh, no. That's just terrible."

"It certainly is."

Tate stood and came over to chat with Millie.

"Why would they do that?"

Millie turned and stared at Tate. Her head tilted back as far as it would go. "Who are you?" she asked.

Lara's cheeks heated as she realized she should have introduced them. "Oh, I'm sorry Millie. This is Tate Vickers. He's here to work on the base."

Her cheeks burned hot and her chest filled with heat, as she realized she wasn't totally sure what he did out there, but he wasn't working on it, per se.

Tate grinned and chuckled. "I'm actually here to stop the vandalism out at the base. Anything you can share, the better it will be for us."

Millie actually tittered. It was all she could do not to roll her eyes.

"Ohh, well, um." Millie lightly cleared her throat. Her eyes never left Tate's and a rosy color tinted Millie's wrinkled cheeks.

"Well, it wasn't just the old sewing factory. They actually also broke windows at the school and the Lutheran church just out of town. They seemed to focus on the windows and nothing else. Rumor about town is they stuck to the windows because they are just causing trouble but not enough to get thrown in jail."

"But why?" Tate asked.

Millie shrugged her older shoulders and smiled. "That's the million-dollar question, Mr. Vickers."

His eyes darted to hers and held for a few moments. Butterflies swirled in her tummy.

Her father stood abruptly and knocked his chair over. He jerked his head to the side and bent to pick up the chair, but he never looked her way. Aidyn stood, his shoulders back and his posture rigid; Tate strode over to join the men. Their voices were hushed but harsh.

Tate asked, "Why can't you just be honest?"

Her father's voice rose. "I'm honest..." He glanced her way then inhaled deeply and shook his head. He turned and stomped out the door as Tate and Aidyn watched him.

Her father slammed his squad car door, and she raised her eyes to Tate's as he turned toward her.

Millie tittered. "Well now, that's not very friendly."

Lara sighed. The gossip mill would be busy today.

She smiled. "It's been rather stressful lately, Millie."

"Goodness, that's an understatement."

He leaned closer to Aidyn. "That's a tell."

"It sure is."

He turned and Lara and Millie were staring at him. He smiled and cleared his throat. "If you don't mind, I'll go check your security system."

"Not at all. It came back up around five-thirty this morning."

"I can check the logs to see what happened."

She nodded but her eyes were wary.

He turned to Aidyn, then strode to Lara's office. He shook the mouse on her computer and waited for it to wake up. Aidyn leaned against the door frame and waited.

Logging into the system, he checked through the logs. "Power outage at three-thirty this morning." He scanned the logs and other than the power outage and then the power restoration, there wasn't anything else to point to the issue.

"Addy said she heard the BRR Jeep revving up and down streets last night around two thirty. The power outage here was at two thirty. Lara said when she came to the bakery this morning, the power was off around town and lights were flashing. Seems like too much of a coincidence, don't you think?"

"Yep." Aidyn scratched his jaw and looked over his shoulder into the bakery. "Bennit's a bit touchy today too."

"You think he had something to do with it?"

"Not necessarily the power, but he sure doesn't want to look into it or anything else that has to do with the BRR. I'd like to have a private discussion with the sheriff about Bennit."

He looked into Aidyn's eyes and saw determination. "I think we're on the same page."

He sent the security logs to Spencer, then turned the monitor off. Aidyn turned to leave and bumped into Lara.

"What's going on with my father?"

Aidyn maintained eye contact with Lara but didn't say anything.

Tate stood and Lara turned to look at him. "Lara." He took a deep breath. "There's something between your dad and the BRR. I can't figure it out. Everett hinted at it yesterday when we were up there. Your dad seems especially touchy about the subject and doesn't like being questioned about it."

Her shoulders slumped. "I know."

She turned and drifted into the bakery and slid behind the counter. His stomach tightened as he watched her lean against the glass bakery case.

A quick glance at Aidyn, he jerked his head toward the door. Aidyn strode to the door and waved at Lara as he stepped out of the bakery.

Cautiously, he moved toward Lara and watched as she took in deep breaths.

"Lara?" Her sad eyes looked into his. "What do you know or think about your dad and the BRR?"

Her throat constricted as she swallowed. She squared her shoulders. "I've overheard people talking the past couple of years. They didn't know I was listening. When I came back from college the rumors were thick around here. But, they always are. Some of the old biddies in town were whispering that my dad had a girlfriend up in the hills."

His brows rose into his hairline faster than he could stop them. "Is it true?"

She shrugged slightly. "I don't know. I asked him about it and he told me not to be ridiculous. But..."

She cleared her throat and swiped at invisible crumbs on the glass case.

"I won't say anything, Lara."

Her eyes closed a moment then opened and delved into his. "I've wondered about it over the years. A lot. My parents keep so many secrets. They always have. I've often felt like an outcast in my own home. My mother's illness. My father's comings and goings. The secrets never go away. Even now when I ask what's wrong with my mom, my father tells me not to worry about it."

He reached for her hand on the glass case and wrapped his around it. Her eyes welled with tears, and she swallowed, but he never looked away from her.

He'd been attracted to her right from the start, but right now, her vulnerability was magnetic.

"I'm sorry, Lara. That must be difficult to live with."

She inhaled deeply and cleared her throat. "I'm used to it. But I'm afraid it's made me terribly weird about being left out of things. I've chased more than one boy away."

He chuckled. "They were just sissies."

She laughed. But didn't pull away from him.

"So? I have some weird idiosyncrasies."

Her eyes rounded. "You do not."

"Of course, I do."

"Well, don't leave me hanging. Tell me."

"I love cookies. And, when there's only one cookie left, I can't let anyone else have it."

"Oh, gawd. That's not a weird idiosyncrasy."

"It isn't? I think it is. My brother and sister have always teased me about it. They said I was selfish and wouldn't share. I think my sister said, 'Tate's a non-sharer.'"

Lara laughed and he couldn't stop the grin on his face.

The door opened and Aidyn yelled. "Tate, we have to go. Trouble."

He pulled away. "Sorry, Lara. Talk later, okay?"

He ran out the door before she could respond and jumped into his truck.

"What's the issue?"

Aidyn slammed his door. "Spencer has been hurt at the base."

"What?" He gunned his truck down the road. "What happened?"

"He was hit by the old Ford the BRR drives."

"Is he hurt badly?"

"I don't know. Addy just called and said we needed to get out there."

Tate swallowed the lump in his throat. He was responsible for his team here and he was in the bakery when he should have been at the base where his team was. He'd forgotten his place here. Lara was a distraction to him. He couldn't let that happen again. The last time he'd allowed himself to be distracted a teammate was injured and it took him years to get over the disgust in himself.

He roared through the gates and stopped in front of the office. An ambulance sat a few yards away near one of the smaller building's footings. He took off at a run, Aidyn alongside him.

He saw Addy standing close and ran to her first.

"What happened?"

"Spencer saw the BRR on camera cutting the fence. He went out to stop them, I was a few steps behind. That Ford truck came out of nowhere and stepped on the gas. They aimed for Spencer. He managed to jump out of the way before they hit him. It seems his foot took the brunt of the damage."

He moved toward Spencer. Medics had him lying on the stretcher and were loading him into the ambulance.

"Spencer? Talk to me. How bad is it?"

"Addy thinks it's broken. Right now, the adrenaline is beginning to subside and it's throbbing."

"Did you see who was driving?"

"Yeah. The one with the long blonde hair. They lured us out here, I'm sure of it."

"Where are the workers?"

"Not here yet."

The EMTs pushed the gurney into the ambulance and Tate's phone rang in his pocket.

The mayor's number appeared on the display. "Fuck."

TWENTY

Lara dabbed at her eyes and sucked in some deep breaths.

A customer walked into the bakery and she plastered on a smile.

"Hi, how can I help you?"

She was grateful for the business and the interruption of her dark thoughts. She hadn't told anyone about her fear of being left out except Shianne. And, she knew it first-hand, since that's where Lara spent most of her time as a kid. She felt more included at Shianne's house than her own. Shianne and her parents treated Lara as one of their own. They'd given her more love than her own parents had.

She went through the motions of the day. Baking and taking care of customers as they came in. She finally had a minute and called Shianne.

"Hey, there. I hear you've been busy today."

"How did you hear that?"

"Lara, we share many of the same customers. Remember, there's only about twelve hundred people in this town. Good gravy, how do you even have to ask that?"

She gave her head a sharp shake and paused to get her thoughts in order. "Something's up with my dad and the BRR."

"You mean something more than usual? What's happened that you finally want to see it for what it is?"

"Tate and…" She cleared her throat.

"Tate? You've been seeing him a lot these days."

"He was here." A car drove by and she watched it pass. "This morning. I mean, he and Aidyn were here to meet with my dad."

"Oh, now that's interesting. What happened?"

"I don't know. He raised his voice—my dad. He raised his voice a couple of times then realized people could hear and lowered it. I couldn't hear anything. Tate wouldn't really tell me anything. We were having a conversation then he was called away. It's…I told him…"

"I heard the ambulance was called out to the base."

"Oh no. That's terrible. Do you know what happened?"

"No. Not yet." Shianne's voice lowered. "You told Tate what?"

"About my parents and their secrets."

"Oh, wow. How did he take it?"

"He made me laugh with a story about being weird about cookies or something. But we didn't get to finish our conversation. He got called away."

"I'm sorry, Lara. I know that was hard to admit. You've kept that to yourself for the most part."

"I told you."

"I know. But I mean you haven't told anyone else."

Lara stared out the window for a few moments then sighed. "No. It's embarrassing, to be honest."

Shianne chuckled. "Why are you embarrassed? Your parents should be embarrassed."

"I guess."

"Hey, are you alright?"

"Yeah. I just needed to hear your voice. It's been a weird day."

"Yeah. Lately they're all weird with the BRR creating havoc. I think they tried getting into my shop last night. The locks in the back are scratched up like a screwdriver or something was used on them. My dad just came and changed the locks for me."

"Oh no." Lara sank against the counter near her coffee machine. She watched the mailman leave mail in her box near the road and started toward the front door. "I'm sorry to hear that Shi."

"They didn't get in, so there's that at least."

She sauntered to her mailbox. The outside air was clean smelling and warm. Her shoulders relaxed slightly and she decided she should sit outside and enjoy the beautiful weather a bit more. Maybe she was letting the BRR keep her cooped up and scared and that wasn't good for her mental health either.

"I just stepped outside to get my mail. Shi, we need to sit outside and have a drink after target practice tonight."

Shianne laughed. "That sounds fantastic."

"Good." She pulled the front of her mailbox open, pulled her mail out and closed the door. As she walked toward her bakery, she saw the first letter on top. "Shi? I got an insurance check. Oh, I'm so happy."

"That's great Lara. We'll celebrate that tonight too!"

"Sounds good. I better go and get some cookies in the

oven. I'll see you around six at your place. We'll practice, then go back to your place and enjoy the outdoors."

"Sounds like a plan. See you then Lara."

She pocketed her phone and inhaled the fresh air before stepping inside.

Straightening the chairs at the tables, she looked around her bakery and a new sense of pride lifted her spirits. She was letting all this weigh her down. She'd stop that. She was fortunate in so many ways.

She slid more cookies in the oven, removed the cooled cookies from the baking sheet they rested on and bagged them up for freezing.

Her doorbell rang and she walked into the bakery to see a woman she'd never seen before. "Hello, how can I help you?"

The woman looked around the bakery. Her clothing was clean but unusual. Her hair was graying but tied back in a bun at her nape. Her eyes were light blue, close to the color of her father's eyes. She looked older than her parents, maybe in her late fifties. No makeup. No jewelry.

"I just came in to see. I've not been here before."

"Oh, feel free to look around. I have fresh banana muffins in the case. I still have two loaves of cinnamon bread at the end of the case. And, I still have two loaves of breakfast bread left."

"What's breakfast bread?"

"Oh..." Lara walked to the end of the case and pointed to the loaves. "It's filled with a sausage blend and cheese, braided, and baked. It's an entire breakfast baked together."

The woman stared into the case for a long time. "It looks good."

"Would you like one?"

She shook her head, then stood and stared into her eyes. "I'm only here to tell you I'm sorry. My boy helped wreck your place the other day and I'm very sorry for his behavior. He wasn't supposed to do that. But those boys together are just no good."

Chills ran the length of her body. Her throat dried and her stomach knotted. "You're from Hickory Hills?"

"I am." She smiled slightly. Nodding she turned and walked to the door. When she stepped outside, she waved and smiled.

Lara watched her walk across the parking lot and turn up the road. She stood frozen in place for a long time. The ringing in her ears grew to the point of deafening. Her arms and legs felt like lead when she locked her door.

TWENTY-ONE

Tate sat in the construction office while Baxter finished a call with a friend.

Baxter ended his call. "Okay. My friend will be bringing several shipping containers later today. We'll situate them from the base of the hill, and across the entire expanse of open ground. We'll leave enough room for the dump trucks to come in and leave, but when not in use, one of the excavation machines will be blocking the opening. He said he has enough containers that we can nearly surround the open areas. We'll set them in front of the fencing and put them tightly together so they can't be walked through."

Baxter scratched his jaw. "I'm not opposed to putting electric fencing around the containers either. I've had enough of these BRR bastards. Today, that was the last straw."

"I agree. Luckily, Spencer wasn't hurt worse than he is. He's bruised, nothing broken. But he'll be on crutches for a while."

"I thought Addy said his foot was broken."

"She thought that. Turns out, his ankle was badly sprained. It was too swollen for her to confirm without X-rays. He'll need to stay off it and therapy, but he'll be fine."

"Okay. So, moving forward, we'll have the perimeter surrounded with shipping containers. What have you managed?"

"I've called my contact at the DoD. He's authorized the capture of any of the BRR found on the base grounds. If we don't get cooperation from the sheriff, we'll need to construct a place to hold them until the DoD can get here to transport them to a military installation. I'm going to meet with the mayor in a few minutes, since I missed my meeting this morning. Then, I'm going up to speak with Everett once again."

"You'll take backup with you, correct?"

"Yes. Aidyn will come with me and I'll have Henry and Maya on standby and close."

"Sounds good. I'll direct the containers to be placed while you're at your meetings."

"Thanks Baxter. I think we've got a good plan moving forward."

Tate exited the construction trailer and walked across the grounds to where Aidyn stood lookout while the electrical crew laid new wiring down. Pulling up his phone he tapped Henry's picture as he walked.

"Delany."

"Henry. I need you and Maya back out here. Aidyn and I are going up the mountain in an hour and I'd like you and Maya close and ready in case we need assistance. Bring communication devices with you when you come out."

"You got it."

He looked into the basement where the men worked. Aidyn asked, "Have a plan?"

"Yep. We're going to meet the mayor then we're going back up the mountain to talk to Everett and tell him we'll be taking prisoners."

Aidyn laughed. "Now we're talking."

"As soon as Henry and Maya get here with our comm devices, we'll go up. In the meantime, let's go chat with the mayor."

The drive to the mayor's office was quiet. Tate's gut tightened every time he thought about Spencer and his close call. He should have been here.

He swallowed a few times, unable to wet his throat. He pulled into the gas station on the corner. "I'm grabbing a water. Do you want something?"

"Nah."

He trotted to the truck with his water in his hand, twisted the cap from his bottle and drank down a third of the cold liquid. He could feel it slide down his throat and he hesitated a moment to let the feeling wash over him.

Settling his water bottle in the drink holder he moved from his parking space and toward the mayor's office.

Once in the parking lot, he glanced at Aidyn, who grinned. "Let's go tell him how this is going to go."

Tate nodded and opened his door. They walked in unison to the front door. Entering the building the receptionist asked, "Do you have an appointment?"

"We do. Tate Vickers and Aidyn Dunbar to see Mayor Rayleigh Winters."

The receptionist giggled. "He prefers Ray. I'll let him know you're here."

She picked up her phone and pushed a button. "Ray, Tate Vickers and Aidyn Dunbar are here to see you."

She hung up and pointed to a door at the end of the hall. "You can go in, he's ready."

Tate nodded and hurried to the mayor's office. He knocked twice before opening the door. Mayor Rayleigh Winters was a man of moderate height. Tate and Aidyn both bent their heads down to look him in the eye. He had a quick smile on his face, wore glasses, and had a spare tire around his middle.

"Nice to meet you, Tate." He vigorously shook Tate's hand then Aidyn's. "Aidyn, nice to meet you."

He pointed to two green upholstered chairs in front of his desk. "Take a seat and call me Ray."

After sitting, Ray walked around his desk and sat in his chair. "Tell me what's on your mind."

Tate leaned back and crossed his left ankle over his right knee.

"I assume you've been apprised of the situation today with the BRR and my teammate Spencer Lawson."

"Yes. How is Spencer?"

"He's fine. Sore. Pissed."

Ray nodded his head and folded his hands together. "It's my mission while I'm mayor to extract the BRR from Hickory Hill, or more properly, Sugar Maple Mountain."

"How are you planning on doing that?"

"I'm in a situation here, Tate. I have to tread carefully as some of the town council aren't on the same page as I am. Getting them to recall the tax deferment was a big step. Even that was only won by one vote."

"And after that?"

"Well, when they can't pay the taxes, we can have them removed. I'll call the governor and ask for assistance from the National Guard."

"And, you're aware that the townspeople are afraid that will lead to an all-out war."

Ray sat back in his chair and rubbed his jaw. "I'm aware. And it just might be the cleansing we need for the town."

"By cleansing, you mean loss of life?"

His right shoulder rose and fell. "Sometimes that's what it means."

Aidyn let out a breath. "Why is Officer Bennit soft on the BRR? And why doesn't the sheriff force him to get tougher with them?"

"Yes. The sheriff is in the leave-them-alone camp. They largely let them cause trouble and wreak havoc thinking they're getting back at those of us who want them gone. All they're doing is solidifying our position that the BRR is nothing but trouble."

Tate dropped his foot to the floor and leaned forward. "What have you heard or do you know about men going up the mountain and sampling the women up there?" He raised his fingers in air quotes. "That's Everett's complaint and wording, not mine. And he further told me to ask Officer Bennit about it."

Ray frowned and nodded slowly. "I've heard rumors."

TWENTY-TWO

Lara pulled into Shianne's driveway and heaved out a deep breath.

Shianne motioned to her from the side door. "Let me grab my range bag and lock up."

Lara looked up into the sky and closed her eyes. The sun wasn't high in the sky at this time of day, but it was still warm. She inhaled the fresh air. Lilacs and wisteria.

"Are you smelling the air?"

She smiled at Shianne. "I sometimes let myself forget about all the beauty we have here. I've been dwelling on the bad that's happening. I've been letting myself drown in my own problems."

"I think we all do that Lara. We both know I've had those times too."

She giggled as they walked to her car.

Once they'd buckled up, she pulled out of the driveway and headed toward the edge of town.

"So, I had one of the BRR women in my shop today."

Shianne's head whipped around. "What? No way!"

"Yes. She apologized for her son's behavior. He was one of the boys, men, whatever, who wrecked my place."

"Which one? Whose Mom is she?"

"I don't know. I don't know any of their names or who they belong to."

"Did you tell your dad?"

"No."

"Tate?"

"No."

"Lara, you need to tell someone."

She shrugged her right shoulder as she turned a corner. "I'm telling you."

"No, I mean...great, but you need to tell someone who can watch things for you."

She bit her bottom lip but said nothing. She turned onto the dirt road that led to the outdoor shooting range.

"What did she look like?"

Lara shrugged again. "I don't know. Her hair was pulled back into a bun at the nape of her neck. She wore plain clothes, no make-up or anything. But, she was clean and she smiled."

Shianne turned to face out the windshield. A quick glance told Lara her mind was spinning.

She found a parking spot and pulled in. They both sat quietly for a few minutes then Shianne asked, "Did she look around?"

"A little. She looked at the baked goods and said they looked delicious. She asked what breakfast bread was and I told her. Then she apologized and left."

"And you don't think she was casing the place or anything?"

She swallowed as she stared into Shianne's eyes. Licking her lips she shrugged. "I don't think so. She looked at the bakery. She complimented me on the break-fast bread, apologized, and left."

"And I wonder what was going on while you were there with her. She was likely there to keep you occupied."

"That's crazy. Anyone who knows me knows I'm at the bakery every day until around four. Sometimes later than that. I went home after work to get my range bag and nothing was out of place. I had to lift my garage door by hand because I had unlatched it to get out this morning."

"Hmm." Shianne opened her door and stepped out without another word. She opened the back door and pulled her range bag out.

Lara did the same. They walked in unison to the office.

An older lady was behind the counter. "Evening ladies. You need to sign in."

Shianne signed in first. "Are you both members out here?"

Lara smiled at her and pulled her membership card from her wallet. "Yes, ma'am." She handed her card across the counter to the lady and stepped up to the book after Shianne stepped back.

The lady laid her membership card on the counter in front of her and took Shianne's card and examined it. Lara tucked her card into her wallet and shifted the weight of her range bag to her opposite shoulder.

"Alright. Go on through." She held a buzzer which opened a back door for them to step out on the range. The smell of gun powder was strong the instant they stepped outside. The loud popping of gunfire from the separate areas of the range filled the air. Shianne pointed to two empty spaces in front of the targets, and they walked to them. Setting their bags on the table between them, they opened their bags, pulled their guns from inside and loaded a magazine. Lara tucked her electronic ear plugs in her ears and slipped her safety glasses on.

She took a few deep breaths to steady herself. For some reason she always got nervous just before firing. She waited for her body to calm, raised her gun to the target in front of her and steadied her breathing once more. Then, she aimed at the middle of the target, let out a slow breath, and slowly squeezed the trigger. Once the first bullet was fired, she fired again and again, emptying her magazine of twelve bullets then looked at the target. She smiled as she saw her aim was still spot on, then glanced at Shianne's target and saw her friend was still a crack shot. They'd grown up out here. Practicing weekly after they'd first gotten their guns for their fourteenth birthdays. Both sets of parents had discussed it and since they'd been practicing and had shown responsibility, they'd each gotten pistols. Man, they thought they had the world by the ass when they came out here the first day with their very own guns.

During college, they didn't practice as much, but they still managed at least once a month. Then they both worked at their respective businesses and time slipped away some days. But, her shoulders relaxed now and her heart beat steady and ready. When she turned to look at Shianne, both women smiled. They were on the same page with this.

TWENTY-THREE

Tate and Aidyn found themselves driving up the mountain road closest to the base. Henry and Maya watched them from the trailer. Several shipping containers had been placed this afternoon, more were on the way. It was beginning to look like a fortress. From this vantage point, they could see down into the nearest part of the base, but the trees and brush obstructed much of it.

He looked at Aidyn. "Think they're waiting for us?"

"If not waiting, they're watching."

"I suppose they'll be all hot and bothered about the containers."

Aidyn laughed. "Likely. That makes me happy."

Tate chuckled. "Me too."

A glint to his left caught his attention. "There they are."

"Yep."

Three four wheelers pulled out of the brush and blocked the road. He put his truck in park and exited. He strode toward the three men, two of them the same as last time.

The one in the center he recognized as the man who drove the Jeep and shot at his truck. That man's eyes glanced at the top of Tate's truck and a slight grin spread across his face. It reminded Tate of the Grinch. Slow. Creepy. Evil.

He had dark hair and blue eyes. He looked like someone Tate knew. It was likely his face was permanently imprinted in his mind because the fucker shot up his truck.

"And to what do we owe the pleasure today?" One of the men said.

"We're here to see Everett."

"Again? What makes you think he's interested?"

"I've got some updates. He's interested."

The three chuckled and kicked at the ground a bit. From his peripheral vision, Tate saw Aidyn look at him then stand taller, his chest puffed out and his hands were ready to draw if need be.

The man standing to the right of the three glanced at the younger man in the middle and tossed his head toward the mountain. "Kent, go 'announce' our visitors and see if President Howard will accept them."

The younger man spat on the ground between them, a glare in his eyes. Tate had a weird déjà vu moment and rotated his shoulders.

Kent scowled once more, then hopped on one of the four wheelers, started it and moved as fast as it could up the road, disappearing around a corner.

His eyes then landed on the older of the two standing before him. "As I mentioned, my name is Tate Vickers. This here is my teammate, Aidyn Dunbar."

"And?"

"What are your names?"

"What's it to you?"

Aidyn's anger boiled to the surface. Tate could feel the anger rolling off him. When he spat out his words, it was clear just how close to boiling he was. "What's wrong with being friendly?"

The older man chuckled, then shrugged. "My name's Brenner. His is Ramsey."

Tate nodded. "It's nice to meet you."

His phone buzzed, and he pulled it from his pocket and tapped the icon to answer. It wasn't lost on him that both Brenner and Ramsey flinched.

"Vickers."

Spencer's voice said, "Keaton Bennit wants to know if you're up in Hickory Hills trying to meet with Everett Howard."

"Yes, I am."

"Okay. What do you want me to tell him as to a reason?"

"Not a thing. We'll be taking care of things from this point forward."

"Okay." Spencer chuckled. "I love how big your balls are, Tate."

Tate chuckled. "We'll see how big they are when I get back."

Spencer chuckled. "I'll let him know."

Tate ended the call and tucked his phone into his front pocket once again. Ramsey and Brenner stood in their spots, but they fidgeted and kicked at the ground a bit, and he wished he were in their heads. He wasn't sure if they were unpredictable or when confronted, were like most bullies, and shrank back because they weren't expecting confrontation. He'd bet the latter, but he wouldn't stake his life on it.

The sound of the four-wheeler barreling down the hill grew louder and his heart beat faster as it neared.

Kent stopped just behind Brenner and Ramsey and dismounted. He looked directly into Tate's eyes and his mouth contorted, as if what he was about to say had a bitter taste.

"President Howard will see you. You'll need to walk up the rest of the way."

"We're aware."

He glanced at Aidyn who shook his head but started following the three assholes from the BRR, who rode on their four wheelers ahead of them, kicking up as much dust as they could.

As soon as they were out of sight, he turned his comm unit on and Aidyn did the same. He called down to his teammates. "We're on foot. Heading to see Everett. He must have a phone up there. Someone called Bennit to tell him we were up here."

Henry responded. "That's rather interesting. Maybe Addy should go sit with Keaton Bennit and watch him."

Tate thought for a moment. "I don't know about that. For the time being, I'd like Bennit to be unaware that we know he has a direct line of communication up here."

"Roger."

They made their hike without further talking. It was warm outside, and he began to sweat. Every so often, one of the three men would stop and look back at them, making sure they were still walking. He hoped they were also at least slightly impressed with the fact that he and Aidyn were in pretty good shape and made the hike look fairly easy. He reminded himself again to put hill climbing on his workout. But he silently hoped he wouldn't have to make this trek that often. He felt vulnerable and uneasy up here in their territory. They were armed, but so were the BRR. And the BRR were, at best, unpredictable.

Finally nearing the clearing he remembered from before, he saw a few people moving around, performing everyday tasks. One woman made clay bowls on a table made of rough logs, tied together with strips of rope. Her hands were deft, her fingers easily molded the clay into different shaped bowls and accessories. The piece she worked on now seemed to take the shape of a pitcher. Her thumb and forefinger smoothly formed the spout. It was impressive watching artisans work.

"Quit gawking." Brenner groused.

Tate leveled a harsh look on him, which seemed to get the point across. Brenner turned and kept walking toward the same cabin they'd stood in front of yesterday.

Before they reached their spot in front of the porch, Kent jogged to the cabin and knocked three times.

Everett exited his cabin looking every bit the imperial he thought himself to be. His clothing was different but similar, the long squirrel tail vest the same.

"I'm trying to figure out what you'd need to talk about again today. If I didn't know better, I'd think you liked coming up here."

Tate and Aidyn said nothing and Everett stared at each of them. Trying to make them squirm didn't work so he began talking.

"Alright." He heaved out a big breath and tucked his thumbs into pockets sewn into his vest. "Let's hear what's so important that you've made the trip up here again twice in as many days."

"I'm sure you're aware that we're installing shipping containers on the perimeter of the base. I've been given permission from the United States Department of Defense to take prisoners of anyone who trespasses. Or causes any damage. We'll be doing that effective immediately."

Everett stared at them. His eyes took on a sinister leer and Tate's heartbeat increased as his mind began running all scenarios through his head.

"If you take any of my people hostage, we'll come down guns blazing to get them back."

"We'll be ready for you, guns blazing."

Aidyn chuckled slightly and Everett's eyes landed on him. Aidyn grinned at Everett before saying, "We've fought in real wars, Everett. We've battled enemies you've never dreamed of. We'd prefer not to fight, but we will. With all we have."

The silence grew between them and Tate wondered if they should just turn and leave, but he wanted to know about Keaton Bennit.

"What information do you have on Keaton Bennit?"

Everett laughed. "Now you want information from me?"

"I think we can help each other."

"Yes. I believe you promised to speak to the mayor about the deferment."

"I asked you to keep your people up here in good faith. You didn't do that."

Everett waved his hand around. "These boys are harmless."

"Then keep them up here."

Everett walked around the railing on his porch to the steps and descended them. He stopped directly in front of

Tate. Close enough, Tate could smell him. He smelled like medicine or joint cream.

"I told you yesterday, reinstate a lifetime deferment on the taxes and we'll talk."

"And I told you to keep your people up here so my negotiations with the mayor would show your good faith. You let them come down last night and disrupt the power, root around the town, and damage property. That's not good faith."

"That's a taste of what will happen if the deferment is not reinstated."

Tate nodded. "Okay. I'll let the mayor know. But we'll be taking hostages effective immediately. The United States government doesn't take kindly to your terrorist actions."

Everett's lips thinned as he looked at the three men standing near them.

He nodded slightly then turned and walked up the steps to his cabin and disappeared inside.

"Let's go, assholes." Brenner spat.

Tate glanced at Aidyn and nodded. They followed two of the men from the cabin with Kent, the third, behind them. They passed through the clearing and to the road they'd come up. As soon as they were just out of sight of the clearing, Kent walked up behind him and shoved him.

Tate caught his balance and whirled around, his hand on his gun at his waist.

"You're just trying to get us in trouble, fuckers."

"No, we're trying to stop the harassment of the townspeople."

Kent stepped forward. "Fuck you and that little bitch at the bakery. That's why you're really here, isn't it?

We've seen you there every morning. She thinks she's so much better than us."

Chills skittered down his spine. They'd been watching. The bakery most likely, but now he was on their radar.

"You tell your president, if he'd like to discuss this, he can contact Keaton Bennit, since he seems to have a phone or a way to do so, and make an appointment with me."

Tate stepped back, unwilling to turn his back on these assholes, and Aidyn did the same. They walked around the two standing in front of them and made long strides down the road.

As soon as they were near the truck, they jumped in, and Tate backed down the hill using only his mirrors.

Aidyn laughed. "Oh, that was priceless."

"Yep. And did you smell him? He's feeling his age I'd say."

"That might make him a bit unpredictable."

Aidyn nodded. "It might. It might also make him vulnerable."

TWENTY-FOUR

Tate dropped Aiden off at the gate and drove to the bakery.

The late afternoon light shining through the windows cast a deep glow on the glass tabletops and the bakery case, giving it a completely different feel than it had in the morning.

At the sound of the doorbell, Lara entered from the kitchen, wiping her hands. "Hi. Long time no see."

Tate nodded. "Yeah, I've been working."

"Of course. Can I get you anything?"

"I actually came in to…"

The sound of tires on the pavement outside had him turning. Keaton Bennit pulled into the lot. "I'm stepping outside for a moment."

"Okaaay." She tossed her towel onto the display case.

Stalking across the bakery, he stepped outside, his jaw clenched tight, hands balled into fists.

Keaton looked up at him as he approached. "Why did you go up to Hickory Hills?"

"That's none of your business. How is it you have a

direct line to their president and you don't stop this shit from happening down here?"

"What makes you think I have a direct line to—"

"I was there when Kent talked to the president, then suddenly, you called my teammate and asked why I was there. That is not a coincidence."

"Tate, you don't know how things work. This is not something you should meddle in."

"Let me tell you what should happen, Keaton. The BRR has broken their treaty. They've shot at a police officer and citizens. They've damaged property and beaten-up citizens. The little assholes *should* be behind bars. The thefts have been going on for years. And you do nothing about it. That's downright suspicious, and now that I know you're in contact with the president up there, I'll go so far as to say, it's downright *fucking* suspicious."

"You cannot go up there again."

"You aren't my boss. I don't answer to you, I answer to the Department of Defense. If you have a problem with me going up into the hills to take care of the bullshit they're pulling, you call them. Until I'm given the word from the DoD to stop, I will do my job. Regardless of whether you're doing yours."

"You don't understand what my job is."

"I'll tell you what you should be worried about. Your daughter." He pointed toward the bakery. "Do you realize Kent and company have been watching Lara? Do you realize he hates her and he's not shy about stating that out loud? What in the fuck are you doing to protect her?"

"That's not true!"

"The hell it isn't. He told me himself. He looked me in the eye and said she was a bitch."

Keaton bit the inside of his cheek as they stared each

other down. Tate wouldn't back down from the man he suspected of being dirty. At the very least, he was not being honest.

He took a deep breath. "What's your interest with the BRR? I won't stop digging until I find out. And, I think I can make a great case for your interference with base construction, which gets the DoD involved in whatever it is you're hiding."

Keaton heaved out a deep breath and looked toward the road. Keaton swallowed then his sullen eyes bored into Tate's.

"Look, Kent is different. He left the BRR three years ago and went to college. He came back from college changed. Determined. He's trying to make changes up there."

Tate shook his head. "No, he isn't. He's causing the most trouble down here. Unless by changes you mean making plans to take over the town."

Keaton laughed, but it didn't reach his eyes. "They wouldn't try that. There are only about ninety people living up there. Many of them are women and children. The numbers don't stack up in their favor."

"Then what change is he trying to make?"

"He wants them to modernize. He wants electricity and plumbing."

"They'll have to pay for that. The lines would have to run up the mountain. That's not going to happen for free. Or for elixir."

Keaton shook his head and moved toward his squad car. "You'll never understand."

"No, I guess I won't. Especially not when I don't have all the facts. You're hiding something."

Keaton turned toward the bakery and flinched. Tate

looked behind him; Lara was watching them from the window.

"She knows you're hiding something too."

"What on earth could I be hiding?"

Keaton stared into his eyes and that weird déjà vu feeling whispered through his body.

Tate whispered, "He's your son."

Keaton paled, and without a word got into his squad car and peeled out of the parking lot. Tate trotted to the edge of the lot and watched the squad car turn up the first road toward Hickory Hills.

He pulled his phone from his pocket and tapped Aidyn's number.

"Yeah. Everything alright?"

"I'm not sure. After I told Keaton off, he left here in a state. He turned up the first road to Hickory Hills without even so much as going into the bakery or making sure Lara was alright. Something very wrong is going on with Keaton Bennit. And I think I know what it is. I think Kent is Keaton's son."

Aidyn whistled. "That's quite interesting. On my way home today, I stopped at Homemade in the Hollow, the little diner on Main Street. The lady who owns the diner told me it's just been this year that Keaton Bennit has gone soft on the BRR. Last year, he was like a pit bull about getting them to stop. She thinks he has a long history with one of the BRR that he's trying to keep secret."

"Right, Kent. Keaton just told me that Kent went off to college and came back changed."

"I couldn't chat any longer with her. Someone came in and she clammed up on me."

"This also explains the rumors that have been going on."

"I think I'll stop by again tomorrow and see if she'll chat with me."

"Good idea. You keep working on that angle. I'm going to work on the fact that Kent seems angry with Lara and I want to know why."

Aidyn laughed, and it rankled his nerves. "He's jealous."

"You might be right. What else could it be? She has the things he seems to want. Keaton said Kent wanted to modernize the BRR with electricity and water and such."

"And what if we send Adelaide and Maya to the dress shop and chat up Shianne? She's Lara's best friend."

"That feels like something that might get me in trouble."

"Not if you aren't doing the snooping."

"I'm staying out of that part of it. I'll be here until she goes home tonight. Did anyone say anything about the electricity being off yesterday? Lara said the power was off all over town. She had to use the emergency opener on her garage to get out of it yesterday."

"I'll check. Be careful."

"You too."

Tate turned toward the bakery and saw Lara still watching him from the window. She looked upset and his guilt of a moment ago washed over him before he could justify his discussion.

He entered the bakery, though he was wary. "What was that all about?"

"Work."

"Just work?" She turned to face him, and he swallowed to wet his throat. "My dad sure took off out of here in a hurry."

"And drove right up the road to the Hill."

Her mouth opened, then closed. Her brows furrowed, and he waited for her thoughts to catch up with him.

"Why would your father go up the hill after an argument? Does he know Kent? And, while Aidyn and I were up there today, Everett Howard called your father and asked why we were up there. Why would he do that?"

"That's not true."

"It's as true as the fact that today is Tuesday."

She swallowed. Pulling a chair away from the little green table. She sat hard in the seat and stared out the window. Just as he was about to sit with her, her phone rang.

"Hi, mom. I'm in the middle of..."

Lara stood quickly and ran to the kitchen. He followed her to see her pulling her purse and jacket from the hook. "I'll be right there."

She looked into his eyes. "I have to go. My mom is sick."

TWENTY-FIVE

Laura sat in Tate's truck, twisting her fingers together. "I could have driven myself."

"I didn't say you couldn't. But you were distraught and I'm still worried about Kent and the BRR watching you."

She exhaled loudly and sat back in the seat.

"How long has your mom been sick?"

"It's been a while now. She's always been prone to sickness. She was sickly. But about twenty years ago, she got worse. Then about four years ago doctors said her heart was slowing down. They didn't say congenital heart failure, but they said her heart muscle was weak."

"I assume she's on medication for it?"

She inhaled. "Yeah. Dad takes care of her medical needs. She was doing so much better until about two months ago."

"Has she seen a different doctor? Sometimes a second opinion is helpful in ferreting out problems."

"Dad said he took her in and adjusted her medication."

She sat up straighter. "You need to turn on the next road."

Tate navigated the corner, and she gathered her thoughts. "Do you think my dad is involved with the BRR? Is that what you were implying earlier?"

He rotated his head on his shoulders. "I suppose it sounded that way. To be honest, I don't know what's going on between your dad and the BRR. But…" He turned to look at her, then licked his lips. "Lara, something isn't right."

She huffed out a breath but said nothing. She pointed to the driveway in front of her parents' home.

"Do you want to come in with me?"

"Sure. If you don't think your mom will mind."

She shrugged. "To be honest, she's too tired to care about much lately."

He exited the truck and walked around the front to her door. It had been a long time since anyone had treated her like a lady. The fact that he cared to do so made her heart swell.

He opened her door and held his hand out for her. She smiled when she looked into his eyes. Since the day she'd met him, actually the day after she'd met him, she'd thought he was handsome. Now, looking into his dark eyes, her tummy swirled. When their hands touched, she felt alive. Goose bumps skittered up her arms and her breathing came in fast spurts.

As they walked toward her parents' home, he took her hand in his and she felt like she did on her first date with Chad Johnson; back in her freshman year in high school, they went to homecoming together. Was it sad that she'd hadn't felt like that since? It was sad for her.

She opened the lid on the keypad on the side of the

garage and entered a code. The door opened and they ducked under instead of waiting for it to open completely.

Tate stepped into the house behind her and she scanned the kitchen. It was spotless. Eerily so, like no one had cooked in it for a long time. That didn't make sense. Her brows pinched together, and she met Tate's gaze. Her shoulders lifted in question.

"Mama?" she called out.

Coughing sounded from the back of the house, and Lara hurried through the kitchen and down a hallway. Tate followed close behind.

Her mom laid on the floor, coughing, as they entered the bedroom.

"Mama. How long have you been lying on the floor?"

Lara tried lifting her upper body to aid her coughing. Tate touched her shoulder, and she stepped aside. He bent and easily scooped her mom up and placed her on the bed. Lara puffed pillows up behind her mom as Tate stepped back.

As the coughing slowed, she sat beside her mom on the bed and motioned toward Tate.

"Mom, this is Tate Vickers. Tate, this is my mom, Laylah Bennit."

"It's nice to meet you, Mrs. Bennit."

She noticed a glass of water on the bedside table and held the glass out for her mom to take. Her shaking fingers held the glass in both hands as she sipped at the water.

"Sorry. Honey. I. Find." She coughed. "Dad."

"It's okay, Mama." Lara looked at the foot of the bed and saw a blanket, but before she could reach for it, Tate swept it up from the foot of the bed and spread it out over her mom. Once again, her heart swelled at his considerate gesture.

Her mom took a few light breaths, then seemed to settle. "Thank you, honey."

"Of course."

Her mom's weary eyes landed on Tate and she smiled. "It's nice to meet you, Tate. Thank you."

"You're welcome, Mrs. Bennit."

Her mom waved her hand out in front of her. Then dropped it to her lap.

"Can you tell me what happened?"

Her mom breathed in and out slowly before responding. "I got scared. I called your dad, but he didn't answer." She took a few slow breaths. "I reached for my medication and dropped it. I fell out of bed. Oddly, my breathing came back, but then I started coughing."

"Okay. I'm so sorry you were scared. What can I do for you while we're here? Are you hungry? It doesn't look like you've started making supper yet."

"I haven't cooked in a week. Maybe more."

Lara's brows pinched together. "Dad said you made stew a couple of days ago."

Her mom only shook her head.

Lara swallowed a lump in her throat. Tate, she noticed, perused the room. Constantly vigilant.

"I can make you some soup, Mom."

Her mom shook her head again, then waved her away with her hand. "I just want to rest now." She scooted down her bed and pulled the blanket up to her chin. Her eyes were closed within a second, halting any further conversation.

She kissed her mom's forehead, then stood. When she looked up at Tate, his eyes locked on hers.

He knelt on the floor, looking under the nightstand and the bed. He sat back on his heels, puzzlement written on his face. "I don't see a medicine bottle."

Lara's brows bunched, then smoothed. "She gets confused sometimes."

He held his hand out for her to proceed him, and after stepping into the hall; he lightly pulled her mom's door closed.

Once they'd stepped back into the kitchen, she turned to face him and felt his warmth wrap around her as he pulled her tightly to him and wrapped his arms around her. She sunk into his warmth and closed her eyes, laying her ear on his chest. She loved how strong his heartbeat was. It was calming. He was calming.

TWENTY-SIX

Tate liked the way Lara felt pulled tightly to him. She fit him, and he liked the way she smelled. He leaned down to kiss the top of her head and inhaled the scent of her hair. She had it pulled into a ponytail today, which showed off her slender neck and the little area behind her ears where he loved kissing a woman. It was soft and warm and usually elicited a response. He really wanted to kiss Lara there.

Lara pulled back and smiled up at him. Her dark lashes framed her blue eyes beautifully. Her full lips curved into a smile and he wanted to kiss them. So he did.

Bending slightly, he touched his lips softly to hers. Her intake of breath was the response he enjoyed most. She always seemed surprised he wanted to kiss her.

Her head tilted slightly, allowing him to cover her lips with his perfectly. He enjoyed moving his lips over hers. With hers. When she opened her mouth in invitation for his tongue to slide inside, he took it.

His left hand slid up her arm and stopped at her jaw.

He softly stroked his thumb along her jaw, and she kissed him back.

He pulled away slightly and lay his forehead against hers. "God, I want you." He whispered.

"I want you too. I don't care if it seems too soon. It feels different with you."

He lifted his head so he could stare into her eyes. They gazed at each other for a long time and the thought ran through his mind that he'd like to stare into her eyes forever. The blue of her eyes did something to him. They made his heartbeat speed up and his fingers itched to touch her. He liked that feeling.

She smiled and whispered. "Why don't we go to my place?"

"Are you sure?"

"I am."

He stepped away and she led him to the back door. They left silently and walked hand in hand to his truck. He held her hand until she situated herself in the seat. He grinned at her and walked around the front of the truck and climbed in the driver's side.

He backed from his parking spot. She giggled. "Can I see your phone?"

He pulled it from his back pocket and handed it to her. He tapped his forefinger on his phone screen to open it and she typed her address and phone number into his phone.

"This way, you'll have it for next time."

"Is there going to be a next time?"

"I sure hope so."

He grinned and followed directions to her place. "Your mom doesn't look like someone with a heart condition. She's thin, too thin. It looks like she doesn't eat. And she has a smoker's cough, but I didn't see any signs of smoking in the house."

"My parents don't smoke."

He thought about her words and the way her mom looked; he'd run it by Adelaide later. If Adelaide wasn't mad about having to dress up for the ball.

The GPS led them to a nice little house two streets behind Main Street. Lara's place was celery green with crisp white trim and a full front porch. A little Cape Cod nestled among ranch-style homes and one other Cape Cod.

"It's cute."

She giggled. "Thank you. I've been fixing it up as I have the time. It needed a lot when I bought it. The inside was dark and the flooring needed to be redone. I've managed most of it. Last year I had the roof replaced. All I have left to do is the basement. It's one of those old stone basements.

"Show me around." He grinned at her.

Her cheeks turned a beautiful shade of pink and his body responded.

After helping Lara from the truck, they walked hand in hand to a side door and entered the kitchen. The white painted cabinets and stainless appliances brightened it up. Her wall decor was exactly like the bakery, all country charm and warmth.

She took his hand. "So, kitchen." She pulled him forward into a room toward the front of the house. "Living room." She turned them back and they passed through the kitchen to a small bathroom, and finally a tiny bedroom at the back of the house."

"Thoughts?"

"I didn't see your bedroom."

She giggled. "I saved the best for last."

She stood on her toes and planted a kiss on his lips, and he immediately pulled her tightly to his body.

Their kiss turned passionate. His breathing came in spurts and her hands roamed his body, making his dick hard. She untucked his shirt, then unbuttoned his pants, lowered the zipper, and her hand slipped inside and rubbed up and down his length.

"God," he whispered.

"Yeah." Her lips kissed his jaw, his neck, then back up to his lips again.

His fingers pulled her top up, and she pulled away long enough for him to slip it over her head.

He quickly pulled her bra straps down her arms, then reached around and unsnapped it. He pulled it away and let it fall to the floor.

Stepping back, he looked at her. Her breasts were beautiful. Her nipples puckered as he watched in fascination, and his hands immediately covered her breasts and molded them gently to his fingers. His thumbs rolled over her nipples and her knees buckled.

"Bedroom," she huffed out.

"Thought you'd never ask."

She took his hand in hers and pulled him to the living room, then to the bedroom at the far left. Her breasts swayed as she walked backwards. The smile on her face was beautiful.

After stepping into the bedroom, which was decorated in blue to match her eyes, she unzipped her pants and shimmied them over her hips. He followed suit, pulled a condom from his front pocket, and let his pants drop to the floor.

"I'm clean, Tate. I haven't been with anyone in a couple of years."

"A couple of years?"

She shrugged and dipped her head as if that embarrassed her. He touched her chin with his forefinger and pulled her head up so he could see her eyes.

"Don't be embarrassed by that, Lara."

"It's just... I guess I just realized how pathetic that sounded."

He leaned down and kissed her lips softly. He ran his tongue over her bottom lip, slowly enjoying the change in her breathing. His fingers found her nipples once more and rolled them between his thumbs and forefinger. Then he kissed his way down her cheek, to her jaw, to that soft warm spot behind her ear and she moaned.

He picked her up, her legs wrapped around his waist, and he took the two steps to the bed and slowly lowered them onto it. He kissed her jaw, then behind her ear again, enjoying the little sounds she made as his lips savored the feeling of her skin against them.

Her hands tugged his boxer briefs over his ass, her fingers moved over the skin of his ass, then up his back, then back down.

She whispered. "Tate."

Her tongue licked the shell of his ear, and his breathing halted. No one had ever done that to him before. She sucked his earlobe between her lips, her tongue flicked it before she moved her lips to his jaw.

He rolled off her, shed his boxer briefs, then quickly tugged her panties down her legs. He hovered over her again and ripped open the condom packet with his teeth.

"Let me." She took it from him.

He groaned. No one had ever done that to him,

either. She rolled him onto his back and straddled his legs. She was beautiful. He leaned up quickly before she started putting the condom on him, and she froze. He pulled the hair tie from her ponytail, and his hands shoved into her hair, wrapping it around her shoulders. It hung in dark waves between them, but his fingers reached behind her locks and once again fondled her breasts.

Her eyes bored into his for a few moments, stunning him with the vision she presented to him. Long dark wavy hair, those light blue eyes. Her lips were pink from his kisses. Her naked body hovering over him. No way could he have been harder. He'd never been harder than he was now.

He rasped out. "Put it on, Lara."

She sat back slightly, her soft fingers wrapped around him, and before she wrapped it in the condom, she pumped his cock with her fist. He felt the pre-cum on the tip of his dick, and her thumb swiped over it and smoothed it across the head, causing him to jerk in her fingers.

A groan started at the base of his lungs and ripped through them as she manipulated his cock. His hands found her legs and squeezed them. "Lara. Babe. Please."

She giggled slightly. She placed the condom on the tip and her hands slowly, painfully slowly, rolled it over his hardened length.

He lifted to roll her over, but she smiled at him, her hands on his shoulders, and nestled him down as she scooted forward and positioned her entrance at the tip of his cock.

He looked down at them, where they were about to be joined, and watched as she slowly lowered herself down his length. His cock disappeared into her warmth, and it was magnificent.

"Argh." He huffed out.

She leaned over him, her hands on his chest, her fingers pinching his nipples and her hips, her glorious hips, worked his dick up and down. If he died right now, so be it. He'd be happy.

He played with her breasts as they swayed before him. His hands dove into her hair. Then he positioned his thumb where they joined, so when she dropped on him, he'd hit her clit.

She gasped and did it again and again. He added pressure and her movements grew faster. He lifted his hips up as much as he could so his cock would drive as deeply into her as he could. She moaned and gasped.

In one swift move, he rolled them over. He drove into her quickly, her pants growing in intensity, until she called out his name.

"Say it again." He husked.

"Tate."

He drove into her a couple more times and his balls drew up painfully, then his seed spilled.

He lowered himself on his elbows above her, his lips against her ear. He kissed her ear softly. "You feel magnificent."

She giggled. "I was thinking the same about you."

Lara kissed Tate before he jumped from his truck to drop her off at the bakery. He looked around at the surrounding area as he opened her door and her shoulders tensed.

They entered the bakery through the back door. Tate walked to the front and looked around to make sure no one was inside, then he returned to the kitchen. Lara pulled a stool to the opposite side of her stainless work table.

"Take a seat and let me make you breakfast."

"You don't have to do that."

She giggled. "I know I don't have to. I want to. Sit."

He grinned as he sat, and she pulled eggs from the refrigerator. "How about an omelette?"

"That sounds fantastic."

"So, while I cook for you, will you tell me about your childhood?"

"Sure. I had a great childhood." He chuckled. "I grew up in a large home, which we call the compound, but which is nothing like a compound. It's an older Southern-style mansion my dad had remodeled to house GHOST. Any of the operatives who want to, live there. The others find homes outside of the compound in town. My teammates here with me, Aidyn, Spencer, Henry, Adelaide, and Maya, all lived on or near the compound. They schooled us on the compound and we all grew up together. We played games like search and rescue, we shot weapons at an early age. Aidyn's mom is a sharpshooter, and she owned a gun range and gave classes. We all grew up knowing how to shoot."

"Wow. That's so different from my childhood." She cracked six eggs into a bowl and began whisking in some milk. "I'm an only child. My mom has been sick most of my life. I've never understood her illnesses and my parents are very hesitant to talk about it. So I grew up kind of on my own. Until I met Shianne when I was in second grade. After that, I spent a lot of time at her house, and we grew up together. Although we also grew up knowing how to shoot. That's something we have in common."

"Did you always know you wanted to own a bakery?"

"Kind of. It was Shianne's mom, Klaire, who encouraged me to bake. It kept us out of trouble, and I had a knack for it. Then, I found I loved it. When we chatted about college, it was Klaire who suggested I go to baking school. Shianne went to the same college, the University in Lexington, for business. We roomed together and studied together. We did everything together. When we came home from college, Shianne's parents surprised her with her shop. It was her graduation present. My parents didn't want to be outdone, and I think they felt guilty, so they bought me this place. I've paid for everything inside of it, though. But it's a great way to start a business, not being too far in debt."

"That's a fact."

She poured the eggs into the frying pan, added cheese, mushrooms, some green pepper, and bacon and put the lid on the pan, then turned the heat down.

"So your parents own GHOST?"

"Yes."

"And you will one day?"

"I guess that's the plan."

She pulled two plates from the open cabinets and laid them on the table.

Moving to the bakery area, she started a pot of coffee and came back into the kitchen. Before walking around the table, she strode to Tate and wrapped her arms around his shoulders. She hugged him to her tightly and closed her eyes as his scent wafted around her.

When she pulled back, she kissed his lips softly, then tended to their breakfast.

"That was nice."

She looked over her shoulder at him. "It was. Thank you."

He stood and stepped out to the bakery. She heard him pull ceramic coffee cups from the shelf above the coffeemaker and fill them. When he came back to the kitchen, she was flipping the omelette onto their plates. They folded over perfectly, and he chuckled.

"You're a professional for certain. I've never managed an omelet to look like that."

"I'll show you some day."

"Deal."

He set her coffee on the table and she slid his plate to him, then took a stool and sat across from him. He took a bite, and she hesitated while she waited for his response. She wanted him to like it.

"Wow. This is fantastic."

"Thank you." She took a forkful of her breakfast, and they ate while they chatted.

Sleeping in his arms last night had been magical. He was kind and caring and gentle. She wondered what she did to deserve such a wonderful man. She'd never enjoyed sex like she had yesterday. Her fingers wanted to touch him everywhere. And she did. Or at least she tried. He did the same thing, and she prayed they wouldn't get bored of each other.

"What do you have to do today?"

He grinned. "I'm on day shift this week. So, I'll be out at the construction site all day. But, Lara, I mean this, if you see Kent, or anyone else from the BRR, call me. There is nothing going on there that can't wait a minute or two. We're mostly there for the presence and we work in twos. So I can come if they are anywhere near here."

"Okay."

He set his fork on his plate, then reached across the table and took her right hand in his left hand. "Baby, tell me you promise."

She swallowed and blinked rapidly because tears threatened. No one had ever called her baby. And no one had ever looked after her like Tate did. Her nose stung as the tears pooled and she inhaled deeply, then let it out.

"I promise."

His fingers squeezed hers.

"Can you promise me something?" she asked shyly.

"Sure." He grinned and waited.

"Will you promise to always call me baby?"

He laughed. "I promise."

He stood quickly and moved around the large table. As he reached her, she stood and his arms scooped her into a tight hug; his lips on hers, their tongues danced and played and when he set her down on the ground, he whispered, "Baby."

TWENTY-EIGHT

Lara hummed throughout her day. The sun was shining; the birds were singing, and, at the moment, all was right in her world.

She was happy when the front doorbell rang, because Tate had set that up. Once again, she marveled at all he'd done to help her in such a short amount of time.

Klaire Brown walked to her glass bakery counter with a huge smile on her face. "I understand there's a man in your life."

Her cheeks burned bright red, and there wouldn't be any denying anything with Klaire.

"It's new."

Klaire reached across the counter and took her left hand in her hands. "Honey, I'm so happy for you. Now, we just have to find a man for Shianne."

"Well, didn't she tell you she was going to the Ball with one of the new guys in town?"

"She did not."

"I'd feel bad about saying anything, except I know it was Shianne who told you about Tate."

Klaire giggled. "I've been pestering her to no end. The talk is all over town that his truck was in your driveway all night last night."

Lara's hands flew to her cheeks in an instant. "Small towns suck sometimes."

Klaire laughed. "Sometimes they do, sometimes they don't."

Lara inhaled deeply to get her breathing under control.

"Now, I'd like a dozen cookies to take with me to the Ball Committee meeting."

Grateful for something to do with herself, she immediately began boxing up the cookies, taking extra care to arrange them nicely.

"Mrs. LeBeau called me for cookies for the ball. I appreciate the order."

"Oh, of course. I'll let her know. She loves your cookies. We all do. Plus, with the troubles of late, we wanted to make sure you're supported."

Lara smiled at Klaire. This woman had been more of a mother to her than her own most of the time. "Thank you, Klaire. I don't know if you'll ever know how much you mean to me."

Klaire, who looked so much like her daughter, smiled at her. "Honey. We've always loved you. Just like Shianne."

Lara walked around the counter and hugged Klaire. "Thank you."

Klaire squeezed her tightly, then kissed her cheek.

"Now you enjoy that new young man you have. I can't wait to meet him."

Her cheeks heated again, but she said nothing in

response. Klaire picked up her box of cookies and left the bakery.

She watched out the big front window, and that's when her blood chilled. Kent sat in the Jeep on the road in front of the bakery, watching. In plain sight.

Lara watched Klaire get into her car, then she walked to the front door and locked it. She pulled her phone from her pocket and called her dad first.

"Hey, honey."

"Dad. Kent's here. He's sitting out front in his Jeep watching the bakery."

"Dammit. Lock the door. I'll be right there."

"I did. Hurry."

Her fingers shook as she dialed Tate's number.

"Hey, baby."

She smiled, but it was gone in a second. "He's here. Kent. He's out front watching the bakery."

"You're shitting me. Lock the door. I'll be right there."

The line went dead, and she felt her side where her gun rested. Tate had insisted this morning that she wear it and she had to admit, right now, she was glad she did.

She peeked out the window; Kent was still sitting on the road, watching her. Or, at least, her bakery. She tried keeping herself hidden so he didn't see her watching him.

Suddenly the sirens sounded, and her father's squad car pulled in behind Kent. Kent gave her the finger out his window and took off. Her father took off after Kent and her stomach twisted into tight coils.

Tate's truck sped into the parking lot and she almost worried he wouldn't stop in time. He jumped from his truck and ran up the steps to the door. She unlocked it as quickly as her shaking fingers would allow and the instant he stepped in, his arms wrapped around her in an embrace.

"Is that your dad's sirens I heard?"

"Yeah. He pulled up behind Kent. Then Kent gave me the finger and took off. Dad chased after him."

"Okay." Tate filled his lungs with air, and she stepped back a bit.

"I'm sorry. I wasn't sure how fast Dad could get here. I was so scared."

"Baby, don't worry. I told you, there's nothing so important at the site right now that I can't take a few minutes. Aidyn is out there, covering. It's all good."

Within a few minutes, her dad's squad car pulled into the lot. He got out of his car, opened the hood and looked inside. After a moment, he shook his head then closed the hood. Tate walked outside and Lara followed him.

"Problems with your vehicle?"

"Yeah." Keaton looked around. "Let's head inside."

As soon as they entered the bakery, her dad kissed her temple, then walked to the coffeepot and poured himself a cup. He turned to Tate and raised his cup. Tate shook his head.

Finally, her dad started explaining. "So, I was chasing Kent and suddenly my car stopped working. It shut down. Luckily, I just navigated a corner and straightened out my squad car or I would have crashed."

"Oh, my god. Dad. You need to call the garage and have it looked at."

"I will, honey. As soon as my nerves calm."

He sat at the little blue table, and his radio buzzed.

"Keaton, we just had a call from three citizens that their cars just quit while they were driving. Two of them had an accident. You're needed at the corner of First and Jackson streets."

"Ten-four. I'm on my way."

Her dad looked up at Tate. "What do you make of that? Everyone's car stopping at the same time?"

"I think it means someone has a way to shut things down, electronically. I wonder if that has anything to do with the power going off yesterday?"

Her dad stood.

"That's certainly something to investigate."

Tate called Spencer.

"Hey, do you still live here?"

"Shut up."

Spencer laughed.

"So, here's something I'd like you to ponder. A while ago, Keaton Bennit was chasing Kent and his squad car shut down. No radio, no siren, no electronics."

"What?"

"Right, so run that through your electronics brain and add in the power outage in town yesterday and the fact that three citizens called the police station, right after Keaton halted his chase, with the same issue. They had an accident because their cars shut down."

"No fucking way!" He heard Spencer moving to another location in the house, he was still using crutches, so it was cumbersome. "Where are you now?"

"I'm on my way back to the base. Kent was watching the bakery, and I ran out to make sure Lara was safe."

"Okay. Let me do some research on this and I'll call you back. Are you coming home tonight?"

"Yes. And if Lara doesn't feel safe, I'm bringing her with me."

Spencer chuckled. "Okay. See you later."

The line went dead and he dropped his phone into his cup holder in the truck. He'd promised Lara he'd pick her up at four today and she complained because she had work to do. They had slept little last night, not that he was complaining. But he'd been up at the ass crack of dawn, and he needed some rest.

He pulled into the construction site and saw Aidyn walking back to the office from the middle of the site.

"Hey. Anything going on?"

"Some cameras stopped working, so I walked out to check them."

"It appears we need to investigate. I'm thinking we need to go up the mountain on foot and in secret."

"What's up?"

Tate motioned to the trailer. He and Aidyn stepped inside and he told him of the electronic issues going on in town.

Aidyn sat back in his chair, his forefinger brushing back and forth across his chin.

"I think those fuckers have a scrambler."

"I didn't think they had electronics up there."

Aidyn sat forward and rested his elbows on his knees. "Tate. They have phones or some communication."

"Yeah." Tate scrubbed his hands through his hair, then down his face. "Fuck, I'm tired."

"Go home. Take a nap. Maya and Henry will be out here soon and I'll be home in an hour. Then we'll chat about what we need to do. Plus, by that time, Spencer might have some ideas of what's happening up there."

"I won't leave you out here alone."

"Bro, you just did. We're fine." Aidyn stood. "It just may be that those assholes have been testing their equipment and now they know it's working. So tonight we'll all need to be on duty."

Tate nodded. "It'll be dark at eight. Maya and Henry will be here. Someone should walk the perimeter, and you and I will walk up the mountain to see if we can find out what's happening."

"That sounds like a solid plan."

Tate nodded. "Alright. I have to pick Lara up at four. I'll set my alarm and we'll make our plan once I get to the house."

"Does she cook?"

Tate shook his head. "She does, but that's not why I'm bringing her Aid."

"I know, but I'm hungry. We've mostly eaten microwaved crap since we got here."

"I'll tell you what. I'll order from the diner and bring it with me when Lara and I get back to the house. We'll eat something good tonight. We can hire someone to come in four times a week to cook for us. How about that?"

"That sounds great. We aren't used to cooking on our own. We've always had Mrs. James and Kylie."

Tate nodded and stood. "You're right. I'll get on it. See you in a couple of hours."

As he drove back to the house, he drove past the streets where the accident happened and noted Keaton was just finishing his investigation. He kept driving toward the bakery to make sure Kent and company weren't stalking Lara.

A block from the bakery, his truck shut off. He slammed on the brakes and grabbed the steering wheel with both hands. Guiding his truck to the edge of the road safely, he took in deep breaths and looked around for anyone lurking about.

He noticed in his mirror the Ford truck he'd seen the first day turn up the road to the BRR compound.

He tried to roll down the window, but the electronics were off, so he opened his door and listened as the engine noise from the truck faded. When he couldn't hear the truck any longer, he turned the key on his truck and it started up.

Grabbing his phone from the holder on the dashboard, he dialed up Spencer.

"Yeah."

"They're scrambling electronics. My truck was just shut down, then I saw the old Ford truck zip up the mountain. As soon as he was out of sight, my truck started again."

"Son of a bitch."

"Right."

"I've been looking at the different codes and waves that can scramble multiple devices at one time and have it narrowed down to three. I just need to know the type of equipment they're using."

"Okay. We'll get that information for you tonight."

"Perfect." Spencer took a deep breath. "So, if they're scrambling, they'll be able to shut down Lara's security system, too."

"That's my next stop. I'll bring her back to the house until we can stop them from interfering with the electronics down here."

"I think the sheriff needs to be aware of what they've been up to. It's an alarming safety scenario. If they can shut down vehicles, even the police won't be able to get to an accident—ambulances as well. Not to mention, if the jail is electronic in nature, they won't be able to keep cells locked. Doors too."

Tate inhaled deeply, then let it out in a whoosh. "I'll pick up Lara and we'll head to the sheriff's office. Why don't you have Henry and Adelaide search for a couple of older vehicles for us to drive? Something immune to their scramblers."

"I'll do that. Be careful."

"You, too. The stakes just got higher."

THIRTY

Lara pulled a pan of cookies from the oven and set them on her table to cool a few moments before transferring them over to the cooling racks.

The lights in the room went out and the soft music playing in the background stopped. Immediately, she felt a sense of dread in her stomach, and she crept forward into the bakery and looked around.

She didn't hear the doorbell but looked around just the same. Then, she opened and closed the door and was met with silence. Her doorbell didn't work. She swallowed the lump that formed in her throat and twisted the lock on the door.

Slowly, she pulled her gun from its holster and held it in front of her. Her hands shook and her heart beat so hard and fast she worried she'd pass out. It made her entire body shake from the force of it.

She stepped to the side of her office door and noted it was slightly ajar. But, she seldom closed it because it cooled off too much and working in there was uncomfortable.

Listening for any movement, her breathing came in shattered spurts and if someone was in there, they'd hear her before she'd hear them. She pulled the door closed tightly and picked up the chair closest to the office and set it in front of the door. If someone was in there, they'd need to push it aside to get at her, and that just might give her the time she needed to get out of the building.

Ambling forward, she stopped just before the utility room door next to the office. It was smaller than her modest office and with the bucket and mop in there, it wouldn't be easy to hide. But determined people did surprising things.

A pounding on her back door made her jump and scream. Grateful she didn't have her finger on the trigger, she scooted passed the utility room door toward the back door. The pounding sounded again, but this time Tate's voice bellowed out.

"Lara. Open up, baby, it's me."

Her shaking fingers opened the locks on the door and as soon as she'd had them unfastened, Tate burst through the door.

He froze when he saw her holding her gun. "Is everything okay in here?"

"I don't know. My doorbell doesn't work and when the lights went off, I walked to the front to see if anyone had come in without me hearing them. I locked the door, but then wasn't sure if someone was in the building or not. I'll be honest, my heart is beating so loudly I wouldn't have heard tap dancing."

"Okay, safely holster your gun."

She swallowed but slowly slid her gun into her holster as asked. His eyes locked on hers. The second she'd holstered her weapon, she threw her arms around his neck and held him close.

His arms wrapped around her waist for a moment, then he whispered, "Let me check the place out and make sure no one is in here."

"Okay."

She stood back and watched as he pulled his gun out and stalked through the building, looking much more comfortable with his gun in hand than she ever would. He moved methodically and slowly from room to room. Before he moved the chair away from her office door, he glanced at her and she shrugged.

He quietly lifted the chair; using his foot, he pushed the door open. With his left hand, he pulled a flashlight from his back pocket and shone it into the room.

Confirming it was empty, he holstered his weapon and sauntered toward her. "It's clear."

"I didn't hear your truck."

"I walked."

"From where?"

"I'm a block down the road. We believe the BRR has scramblers and is interfering with electronic signals. The power signals are huge, but they're also able to stop vehicles from operation and, as you can see, your security equipment, too."

"Oh, my god, that's so scary. What are they after?"

"We're not sure. I've got my team working on some things in the meantime."

"The BRR is shutting down the power?"

"We believe so."

"Oh my god. What about the hospital?"

"They're on generators."

That's when Tate's eyes rounded. He pulled his phone

from his back pocket and tapped a number. "Aidyn, we need a couple of generators. One at the house, one here at the bakery. Before everyone buys them up, I need you to grab them from the general store."

He pocketed his phone again and took her hand. "It isn't safe for you to be here. I need you to come with me to the house where we can protect you."

"Why are they after me? It makes no sense."

"I know it doesn't and for the time being, we just don't know. But I promise to keep you safe until we find out and can stop it."

"Okay." She started toward the kitchen. "I have to turn off the oven. It's gas."

He nodded and followed her into the room.

She turned the knob on the oven to shut it off, then touched the corner of a cookie, to see they'd cooled. As she washed and dried her hands she noticed Tate peering at the side of her fridge. She transferred the swiftly cooling cookies to the rack and covered them with plastic wrap. Who knew how long she'd be away.

Tate pulled away from her refrigerator, then turned to her stove, his flashlight out as he looked all around it.

"What are you looking for?"

"Shut offs. Settings. Depending on the generator Aidyn can find, we may have to run your refrigerator on propane if it's capable. Your stove and oven are fine. I'm just checking."

She took a deep breath and her tummy rolled inside. She was ready for life to get back to normal. And soon!

THIRTY-ONE

Tate helped Lara close up the bakery and secure it as much as they could. Though he tried preparing her for the fact that, just like last time, they could get in if they wanted to. Luckily, she was pragmatic about it. He hoped.

A motor sounded outside the back door and he halted her progress down the hall behind him.

"Stay here a moment."

He cracked the door open and saw Aidyn sitting outside on a UTV from the construction site.

"Your chariot awaits. No electronics on this baby!"

Tate laughed and reached back to take Lara's hand and pull her to the door.

"We won't have to walk after all. Aidyn brought us a ride."

There was a generator in the back dump box and he fist bumped Aidyn.

"Nice work."

"Actually, when I told Baxter what was happening, he opened up a storage container he has at the site and put this one on the UTV. He said to come and get another one later, he has four there. In case one of his goes out."

"Nice. We'll get a couple of them ordered and replace them."

Aidyn drove them to the house and they unloaded the generator. He waved them off. "I can get this set up. You go in and introduce Lara to everyone else."

He took Lara's hand and walked her to the back door and inside the darkened house. Adelaide sat at the dining room table researching something on the internet.

"Hey, Addy. This is Lara. Lara, this is Adelaide Masters. Adelaide is actually our team medic, but she's also a crack researcher."

Adelaide chuckled. "I don't know about crack, but I do alright. Nice to meet you, Lara."

"What are you researching?"

"Spencer asked me to research the three types of scramblers and put together a report on them. I'm using my phone as a hotspot until we get the generator hooked up."

"Aidyn already told you about the generator?"

"Oh, he's all kinds of proud of his find. Actually, Baxter's forethought."

He smiled at Lara. "Lara will be here until we can secure her bakery and her house."

"That's a good idea. One or two of us are always home. You'll be safe here, Lara."

Lara smiled. "Thank you, Adelaide."

Spencer clumped down the stairs. "Hey there, Lara. Nice of you to stop over."

Tate grinned. "Lara's staying here until things settle down with the BRR."

"Great idea."

Spencer stumbled through to the kitchen; the crutches made his movements cumbersome. "Anyone ordering dinner?"

Tate laughed. "I'll order from the diner."

He turned to Lara. "Maybe you can help me find someone who will come in and cook about four days a week. I'm afraid we're helpless in that area."

"I'll cook. I don't mind."

"I didn't bring you here to cook, Lara."

"Well, if I have to be here, I may as well have something to do. But I promise to help you find someone long term."

He leaned in and kissed her lips, and Adelaide grinned behind Lara's back. Lara's cheeks turned an adorable pink, and he liked the color on her immensely.

The lights flickered and then came on, and Adelaide and Spencer cheered.

Tate turned to the kitchen, bringing Lara along with him. "You'll find everything you need to cook with in here. At least, that's what we were told. Whatever groceries you need, call and have them delivered."

He pulled his credit card from his wallet and handed it to her.

"Use this to buy food. You can ask them to keep it on file if they do that."

She smiled. "Okay. So, let me dig right in. What do you want for supper?"

Adelaide called out. "Something besides pizza. I'm sick of pizza."

Spencer turned from digging in the refrigerator. "I have to agree with her. Wings. Meatloaf. Whatever today's special is." He closed the door. "Also, I found a vehicle for us to use. I'm on my way to look at it in a few minutes."

"Sounds good."

She turned to face him. "I'll need to go home and get clothes if I'm staying here."

He smiled at her. "As soon as Aidyn finishes with the generator, the three of us can go over to your place and get what you'll need."

Her cheeks tinted again. "Okay."

"I have to call the sheriff and do a little work. Are you alright here?"

"Yes. I'll be fine. I'll start on grocery shopping."

Adelaide called out. "Oh, we have a showing at the sewing factory tomorrow. We can negotiate the busted-out windows being replaced as long as it doesn't rain and get everything wet inside."

"Perfect. Thanks Addy."

"We need to meet there at nine in the morning."

"Got it. Send a message to everyone."

He walked through the dining room to the living room, where it was quieter, and dialed the sheriff.

"Sheriff Cranford."

"Hi, Sheriff, this is Tate Vickers."

"Hi, Tate. I'm assuming you've heard of the latest electrical issues?"

"Yes, sir. That's why I'm calling. We think they're testing electronics scramblers. I'd recommend you find an older car or two to use until we stop the BRR from disrupting the power grid."

"How old?"

"Old enough that it doesn't rely on electronics to run. No computers on board. We're researching what they're using now and will take action to stop it as soon as we have our information buttoned up. In the meantime, you'll need to look for a generator for the police station, so your computers and systems won't be interrupted at their whim. It may also be a good idea to bring in some police officers or perhaps an advance team from the base to help here, so there isn't mass chaos once the townsfolk figure out what's happening and who's responsible."

"We have generators here, so we're covered. Do you really think it's going to get worse?"

"I think we have to operate under that assumption for safety's sake."

He heard squeaking in the background and imagined the sheriff leaning back in his chair.

"I'll see what I can do about that, Mr. Vickers. You stop those assholes from creating a mockery of our town. They've had it far too easy lately."

"Thanks to your deputy."

Silence. For a few moments. Then his voice was soft. "Yep. I'm aware."

THIRTY-TWO

Lara finished uploading the grocery list on the app for Paxton's Grocery, then turned to see about ordering something from the diner.

She dialed their number and leaned against the counter.

"Homemade in the Hollow."

"Hey there, it's Lara Bennit. I'd like to order dinner to be picked up, please."

"Okay. What can I get for you?"

She tried placing whose voice was on the other end and didn't recognize it.

"What's your special today?"

There was a silence on the other end of the phone and Lara almost asked if she'd heard her.

"Well, we've been having some issues with the electricity, but the Salisbury steak is baking in the gas oven, so that will be done. But we can't get you a fountain soda, because those aren't working. And Abby is worried about the refrigerator, so we'll throw in pies for free if you want them."

"I'll bet the pies will be a big hit here. Thank you. I'll need Salisbury steak dinners for…" She looked into the dining room at Adelaide.

She mouthed, "Seven."

"Seven, please."

"Great. They'll be ready in fifteen minutes. Who will pick them up?"

She shrugged, then said, "Spencer."

She paid with Tate's credit card, then turned to pull dishes from the cabinets. As she entered the dining room, she asked, "Seven?"

"Henry and Maya are at the construction trailer, and someone will run their dinners out to them."

"Okay. Thank you."

Tate entered the dining room and watched her set plates on the table. "Salisbury steak for dinner. Free pie because they're worried about it spoiling and want to get rid of it."

He shrugged. "Bonus."

"And, I said Spencer would pick it up."

Tate grinned. "I'll tell him."

Adelaide looked up at Tate and pointed to her computer screen.

"A scrambler can be uploaded through apps. Somehow they crawl in through apps attached to software. The most common is messenger or chat apps. The easiest way to check is to look at a couple of businesses affected."

"It wouldn't explain the power in houses and vehicles."

"I bet it does. Every business largely uses the same basic word processing systems and they come in a package. So, you'll have a document app, a spreadsheet app, an email app and lately, an internal messaging app. I'd bet that's what they all have in common. If a house has the same software, they'll have the messaging app, even if they don't know it. Who can we ask about this?"

Tate shrugged and Lara said, "What about a point-of-sale app? I don't have a messaging app on my software at the bakery because I have a single license, but most of the businesses use point-of-sale apps. I know Shianne has one in her boutique."

Tate turned to her. "What about the sheriff's department?"

"They do as well. People are always in there paying fines and fees."

Adelaide began typing and reading her screen as she and Tate stared on.

"Yes. Lara's right. Someone can also upload a remote scrambler through point-of-sale apps."

Tate nodded. "Lara, can you call Shianne and ask her what software she's using and what time her power went out—if it did?"

He turned to Adelaide. "You talk to Spencer about this and see if you can drill down the bug they're using. I'll call the sheriff's department."

Lara pulled her phone from her pocket. She decided the kitchen would be quieter for her to chat with Shianne, so she ambled to the kitchen once more. Tapping Shianne's face in her phone, she listened as it rang on the other end. Spencer thumped through, nodded, then kept going toward the stairs.

"Hey Lara. Where are you?"

"I'm at Tate's. Is your power out?"

"It is. It happened a while ago. I've closed the store because I can't cash anyone out."

"Yeah, that's why I'm calling. Tate and the crew are researching some ideas on this and asked me to get the name of the point-of-sale software you use at the store."

"Okay. I'll have to dig in the file cabinet for the exact name since my computer is off."

"What about using your hotspot on your phone?"

Shianne was quiet for a moment, then growled. "I don't know why I didn't think of that."

"It doesn't matter, Shi."

"Okay, the computer is booting back up. In the meantime, Sharon Jackson was in here before the power went out to pick up her dress. She said your mom is sick again."

"Yeah. I don't know what's going on over there. Tate and I went out there a while ago and she had fallen out of bed and was coughing. We put her back in bed and she told us to go. The kitchen was spotless, as if no one has cooked in it for a long time. But you know my parents have been sneaky and quiet about things for a long time, so I don't ask questions anymore."

"I know, honey. I'm sorry. My mom said she came into the bakery today and you looked good. And she just doesn't stop raving about your cookies."

Lara laughed. "Well, that's nice to hear. I always love seeing your mom. She gives the best hugs. And she got me started on baking in the first place, so she gets that credit too!"

"Okay, here it is. It's called PoSTS. Point of Sale Technology Systems."

"Thank you. I'll let Tate and company know."

"Sounds good. So, are you staying there?"

Lara chuckled. "Are you fishing?"

"Yes."

"For a while, until we know I'm safe. Kent has been

watching the bakery. Or me. But he was outside watching the bakery from the road today."

Shianne gasped. "Oh no. What the hell is wrong with that kid? He sure has it in for you."

"I know and I don't know why."

"When you told him you wouldn't trade with him, did something bad happen?"

"No. I didn't even tell him. I told Brenner and Ramsay when they came down. Kent has never been up close to me."

"Was that woman who came in Kent's mom?"

"I don't know. She surprised me when she said 'her son' and I didn't think to ask who her son was."

"Did you tell Tate?"

"Not yet."

THIRTY-THREE

Tate stood from the dining room chair where he and his team sat on their computers. Lara was reading a book in the living room. He smiled when he entered the living room and saw her curled up at the end of the sofa.

"Hi." She smiled at him when she saw him.

"Hi." He sat next to her. "So, Aidyn and I are heading out. I'll be on a mission and unable to answer my phone. If you need anything, Spencer and Adelaide will be here until ten. After that, Maya and Henry will be home. I'm sorry I won't be here to introduce you to them."

She closed her book and set it on the table next to the sofa. "It's alright. I'm a big girl."

He brushed the backs of his fingers along her cheek. "That you are."

She sighed and laid her hand against his on her cheek. He saw her swallow, then he leaned in and kissed her lips lightly.

"I'll be home as soon as I can. You don't have to wait up for me. I'll be quiet when I climb into bed."

Her eyes stared into his, and his heartbeat increased. She really was a beautiful woman.

"Sounds good. Thank you for taking the time to help me get some things from my house."

"Of course. I'm sorry we didn't get the chance to set up the generator at the bakery today, but I promise we'll work on it tomorrow."

"Maybe you'll figure out what's going on and we won't have to worry about a generator tomorrow."

He smiled. "I like the way you think."

She giggled. He kissed the tip of her nose, then stood. "I'll see you later."

She stood and walked with him to the dining room where Aidyn waited for him.

"Ready?"

Aidyn nodded.

Adelaide and Spencer sat at the table with their computers open and she tapped at her ear. "Comm units on."

Tate chuckled. "Yes, boss."

Adelaide shrugged her right shoulder and kept working on her laptop.

He looked at Lara once more, soaking her up before he left on this mission. He was already eager to come home and hold her in his arms tonight.

He turned to walk out the door and the lights flickered. The generator shut off. Turning to Lara, he said, "Will you give Shianne a call and see if her lights came back on? Text me please."

"Sure." She smiled, and he soaked that up too.

As he and Aidyn ambled to the vehicles, he said, "Let's take the old Impala Spencer found for us."

"Sounds good."

As they drove through town, they noticed lights popping on in the businesses.

"This explains why they drive older vehicles. At least one reason."

"They don't have money either."

"True. And that's likely one reason it pissed them off and they're fucking with the businesses in town. It's got to be more than just the trading, or lack of trading. There are still those trading on the side."

He drove into the lot on the construction site and parked next to Henry's truck. They entered the construction office and Henry and Maya sat on their computers, looking at the security cameras around the perimeter.

"What's going on?"

Henry turned and stretched in his seat.

"They came down the mountain on 4-wheelers, and were quiet, which alerted us they were sneaking around. They walked around the fence in the back, approximately two hundred feet. Then turned around and left. I was just about to go out and see if they planted something."

Aidyn shook his head. "Tate and I can walk back there on our way up the mountain."

Maya turned and stood. She pointed to her computer screen.

"They started in this area here. It was Ramsey and Brenner." She started the security video and he and Aidyn leaned in to watch it.

Tate nodded. "Okay. We have our comm units on. They just turned the electricity back on around the same time as this video. I wonder if they did that, so it kept folks busy and not paying attention to what they were doing?"

Henry nodded. "Not a bad thought."

"Okay. We're out. We'll go up the south side of the mountain and see what we can find."

He and Aidyn exited the trailer and stopped at the Impala. They strapped on their weapons, comm units, and flashlights. Then headed across the construction site toward the fence line where the BRR was messing around.

They approached the fence with caution. Neither of the men had bent down as if attaching anything to the fence, but they likely knew they were on camera and would have been sly about their activities.

Neither he nor Aidyn found signs of tampering.

Aidyn walked alongside him and huffed out a breath. "What do you suppose they were doing? It makes no sense."

"It sure doesn't. They seem to be a step ahead of us all the time, which is irritating. And I don't enjoy being played."

"I'm right there with you." Aidyn scratched his head. "So, they came down here and looked around but did nothing. I wonder if Kent was pulling something somewhere else while these two were occupying our attention."

Tapping his comm unit he called out. "Maya, have you looked through the other videos during the same time Ramsey and Brenner were by the fence? We're wondering if they were a decoy."

"I'll run through it now. I've been watching all the cameras."

Exiting the construction site and beginning their trek up the mountain, they walked across large rocks and any path without debris that would make noise. It was likely the BRR was watching them as much as they were being watched.

The sounds of 4-wheelers reached them as they were halfway up the mountain. Aidyn crouched alongside him and whispered. "They're watching. That was a signal. Listen, they're revving their engines in a pattern. Not moving, though. I heard no tires on the gravel."

"You're right." They listened to the alarm, of sorts. Three long revs of the engine, then one short. Pause. Three long revs and a short.

"Let's move around to the southeast side of the mountain. I don't see them using that side as much."

"Ten-four."

They moved along in a crouched position, making their way through brush and trees. The terrain was rugged. More than once, their feet tangled in brush and downed branches covered in leaves and debris.

A soft humming reached his ears. He halted Aidyn and tapped his ear. Aidyn listened with him, then pointed to just above them and to the left. He nodded, and they changed course to see if they could find the source.

A small clearing shone in the moonlight just ahead of them. Within the clearing was a tiny structure, not tall enough for either of them to stand in. There were no windows and only one door was visible.

Both he and Aidyn crouched low and looked for a better vantage point. Footsteps sounded on the dried leaves and brush on the ground. Both stayed low and watched.

Kent stopped at the door of the small structure and kneeled down. Slowly opening the door, he scooted inside. The bluish light that shone from inside was a computer or television screen.

Tate nudged Aidyn. "They have computers in there."

"It looks like it."

"I'd like to get in there and see what they're doing."

"As soon as Kent leaves, we'll head over."

The door opened with a creak, and Kent crawled out, then closed it. He added a padlock to the door and locked it.

Kent slowly ambled up the hill and moved toward the west side. A 4-wheeler started up, and they listened as he motored out of earshot.

Tate moved from the brush they hid in and quietly picked his way to the structure. He circled the outside to see where the wires were located. He noted they were up a tree, then across the tops of the trees then tacked to the nearest enormous tree trunk. Aidyn nodded after he pointed up.

Aidyn followed the power lines to see where they went, and he worked on picking the lock to see what was inside. Several attempts to open the lock failed. "Fuck." He whispered after the third failure.

Finally, setting the pin inside the lock securely, he twisted it open and let out a long breath.

"I'm in."

Aidyn confirmed. "Roger. I'm still following the wires."

Inside, the monitor was off, but he found the power button and turned it on. Of course, he didn't have a password but tried a few he thought might be possible. The fifth try it locked him out. He'd come back with software to hijack their computer.

Turning the monitor off, he scrambled from the structure and locked the padlock once again. Striding across the clearing, he retraced his footsteps to Aidyn.

Aidyn pointed up. "They're running the wires to the base. Hijacking electricity. It makes sense, it's on generator power, so it won't affect them at all when they throw the power."

"I'm sure they have the app worm blocked on their computers."

"True, but sometimes they run amok."

He nodded. "I'm going up further to see if I can see more."

"Right behind you."

They continued up the mountain, slowly making their way, listening intently for any sounds alerting them to others in the area.

Near the top, they started seeing structures. They were the size of small homes and Everett's cabin wasn't within sight from this vantage point. They didn't have plumbing up here, though the townsfolk didn't believe they had electricity either. He and Aidyn continued skirting the structures, careful not to make noise when they heard two men talking.

They froze and listened.

"I told you to stop fucking around down there. You either want to be a townie or you want to stay here with your people."

"I want to be with my people. But I want that fucker to pay. That bakery bitch too."

"You don't decide that. President does. If I catch you going down again, you'll be severely punished. This is your last warning."

Tate's muscles twitched at the remark about Lara. It

had to be Kent, but he hadn't ever heard his voice, so he couldn't identify it.

The two walked away, and one man walked into the structure they now hid behind. They heard items hitting the walls and finally a glass broke. He then yelled, "FUUUUUCK!"

Aidyn slowly rose to look in a window just above them. He stared for a while and Tate rose and looked inside as well. Kent stomped around and paced. Finally, a small older woman entered the structure, which seemed to be their house, and tried calming him down.

"Kent, honey, settle down. You can't keep doing this. You'll be ostracized and I'll be left alone here."

"Mom. Why aren't you mad? How can you not want to kill that fucker and his bitch daughter?"

"He's done nothing to me or you."

"Really? Nothing!"

The older woman sat wearily at an old wooden table.

"He left us here."

"It's complicated."

"And she has everything. I should have a business. I should live the life I want to live. But I'm stuck up here like an orphan. You're left up here working like a dog."

"Kent. Please."

The older woman began crying and Kent stopped ranting and pacing and sat at the table across from her. He said nothing.

Footsteps on the dried leaves startled them and a thin, young woman stared at them. She had long dark hair flowing around her shoulders. She wore a long dress with flowers printed on it and she carried a basket on her arm.

Aidyn looked at her and held his finger up to his lips. Her eyes bounced between the two of them and a barely perceptible nod was followed by her holding her forefinger to her lips. She then turned and walked toward their camp.

"We better get out of here in case she tells someone."

THIRTY-FOUR

Lara donned her pajamas and slid into bed. Tate's bed. It smelled like him. She pulled his pillow to her and inhaled his scent. She closed her eyes and enjoyed the comfort that filled her for the moment. It was close to midnight and Tate was still on his mission. She wasn't sure if that was normal. Hell, nothing in her life had been normal. Not in years, certainly not this past month.

She'd spoken to Shirone twice tonight. She chatted briefly with Adelaide, but didn't want to bother her while she was working. Then Maya and Henry came home and switched places with Adelaide and Spencer.

She closed her eyes again and listened to the sounds of the house. Her shoulders had been tight for days. Kent had wreaked havoc on her life. They'd never had a conversation or any interaction until he smashed her bakery and now he seemed to be stalking her.

Lara heard a door downstairs open, then close, and two sets of feet entering the house.

Her heartbeat sped up, and she scooted to the edge of

the bed. She listened for voices but heard nothing. Then soft footfalls sounded on the steps, and she scrambled to the corner of the room where her clothes laid on the chair.

Gathering her clothing to her chest, she swallowed the lump in her throat and looked around for her weapon. She had it here. She'd left it on the bedside table in the drawer. Looking at the door and the bedside table across from it, she tried getting her brain to focus on what had to happen first. She hated being afraid.

She dropped her clothes and picked up the table lamp by the chair as the doorknob turned. Swallowing the lump in her throat, she raised the lamp above her head, ready to swing it at whoever was sneaking in. Her chest tightened and her breathing became labored.

A man entered the room and the light from the hall showed her it was Tate. She squeaked in relief and he turned toward her.

"Hey, what are you doing over there? Were you going to hit me with the lamp?"

Tears sprang to her eyes, and it took her brain a while to catch on to the fact this was someone she trusted.

Her mouth opened then closed, her eyes grew blurry, and all she seemed to do was clutch the stupid lamp.

He slowly crept across the floor toward her; his eyes showed concern and his voice was low and soothing. "Hey there. It's okay, Lara. Baby, it's me."

His hand reached forward and gently took the lamp from her hands. She blinked rapidly and his handsome face came into focus. She sobbed, then dropped her head into her hands.

He wrapped his arms around her and smoothed up

and down her back. She sniffed then wrapped her arms around him.

"I'm so sorry."

"It's okay. I should have texted you so you knew it was me."

"Oh my God… I feel so stupid."

He moved them toward the bed. He leaned down and pulled the sheets back further, then helped her to lay down. He curled in behind her, his muscular arms pulled her close to him and he held her.

His warmth seeped into her, and she enjoyed his scent as she calmed.

"I'm sorry."

He chuckled, "You have nothing to be sorry for."

Inhaling a large breath then releasing it, she shook her head. "I feel stupid. These past few weeks, everything has been building up in me and I guess I'm tired."

He kissed her head and squeezed her tightly to him. "Understandable. Totally understandable."

They laid quietly for long moments. She warmed in his arms. She rolled over, maintaining as much contact as she could with him.

"I've had so much upheaval in my life these past few weeks. This is all new. Unfamiliar sounds. Bed. People around me."

"I understand, Lara." He kissed her lips, and she wriggled tighter into his arms.

He nipped along her lips. Then kissed her cheek to her ear. His tongue ringed her ear and his deep throaty voice whispered, "You feel so fucking good."

She felt him harden between them and she rocked her pelvis toward him. He responded by sliding his hand down her back to her ass and rocking into her at the same time. She felt how hard he was and pushed back against him. Her hand reached around and pulled him into her again.

He responded by rolling her to her back and scooting between her legs. He began a rhythm of grinding against her, and her body responded. Her nipples pebbled tightly, and she moved back and forth enjoying the friction on them.

Tate's fingers reached between them and undid his button and zipper. She helped him shimmy his pants down his hips until he could kick his feet free. She tucked her thumbs into the waistband of his boxer briefs and shoved them down his hips as quickly as she could. His cock sprang free and pushed heavily onto her clit. He rocked his hips a few more times; the only thing between them was the skimpy fabric of her cotton shorts and the matching cami.

His lips kissed along her jaw, then lower, until he'd grazed a nipple with his teeth. She loved the feeling, hated there was anything between them at all. She pulled on her top until it exposed her breasts to his lips and teeth, and he repeated nipping at her breasts. The cross between pain and pleasure had moisture gathering between her legs as he moved from one breast to the next.

She sighed as his whiskers skimmed along her skin. He was rugged, strong, smart and fucking amazing. He sucked in a breast, as much of it as he could suck into his mouth and she gasped. His tongue flicked a few times and the intensity between her legs grew stronger. Needy. She was desperate right now, and she wanted Tate. In her.

Wriggling her body to let him know she was ready, he

surprised her by rearing back and in one swift movement, he pulled her pajama bottoms off her legs, then bent down and instead of sliding into her, his mouth found her wetness. He licked her and moaned. His tongue found her clit and flicked a few times, but she wanted pressure. She tugged his head close, but he held back, teasing her. He flicked his tongue repeatedly over her clit but withheld pressure. She tried bucking, but he imprisoned her thighs in his firm grip. Her fingers dug into his hair trying to pull him down firmly on her but he chuckled and resisted.

"Tate."

"Am I driving you wild, Lara?"

"Yes."

"Good."

He kneeled on the bed, lifting her bottom as he did. She was so glad the sliver of light from outside lit the room enough to see him stroke his cock a couple of times, then lead it to her entrance. Once seated, he entered her with a thrust of his hips. It was swift, thrilling. His muscles bunched and moved as his arms held her lower body up to his. He smiled as he watched his cock disappear into her and it was the most exhilarating moment of her life.

He thrust in and out a few times, watching the show, then his eyes landed on hers. "You're so fucking beautiful, Lara."

"So are you."

His arms slid from under her and he rearranged himself so he was on top of her. Their bodies joined together. His was muscular and firm, hers soft. The contrast was beautiful and exciting. Each time he pushed himself into her he groaned lightly in her ear. Then he kissed her lips. Firmly, then gently then passionately. The entire dance was erotic and amazing.

He kissed her ear and whispered, "Lara."

She loved the way her name sounded when he said it. Especially when he was inside of her. "Lara."

He ground his hips against her, and she gasped, "Tate."

He repeated that movement over and over until she felt the pressure build to a point of explosion. Her arms pulled him tightly to her, and she whispered, "Tate. I'm going to..."

His mouth covered hers as she shattered. He continued to pump into her, to dance their erotic dance. His movements grew in intensity and pace as she wrapped her legs tighter around him and enjoyed the sensation of Tate filling her in the most intimate way possible.

When he exploded into her, he groaned into the pillow near her ear. "Lara."

She dozed, remembering Tate calling out her name over and over as he came inside of her. Her heart beat wildly as she replayed their lovemaking in her mind.

THIRTY-FIVE

Tate woke to the sweet aroma of—cookies. Oh, what a way to wake up.

He knew instinctively that Lara was no longer in bed. No one in this house could bake and he'd felt her absence in some weird way when he'd rolled over earlier. In his sleepy mind, he knew, but now that he was coherent, he knew!

He showered and dressed and practically ran down the stairs, tracking the smell of vanilla and sugar. As he entered the kitchen, Lara was pulling a freshly baked pan of cookies from the oven and he leaned against the door-frame and watched her. Beautiful. Graceful. And sweet.

She turned and smiled as she set the hot cookie sheet on a rack on the counter to cool.

"Good morning," she crooned.

"Good morning." He stalked forward and pulled her tightly to his body. He smelled her freshly shampooed hair and enjoyed how her body felt pulled tightly into his.

"I didn't hear you get up."

She chuckled. "I'm used to getting up at three in the

morning. I laid awake for a while, but in the end, I hoped you'd all like something fresh-baked this morning."

He chuckled. "I'd like nothing more."

She giggled. "Let me oblige you, then." She tilted her head up and he kissed her lips.

He whispered, "You felt amazing last night."

"So did you." Her eyes bored into his and he couldn't look away.

The timer went off and broke the spell. Her cheeks tinted pink and she stepped away.

She stopped the timer, then donned the oven mitts to pull more cookies from the oven. She added another pan inside and set the timer once more.

"Are you baking two pans at once?"

"I am. I have them separated four minutes apart. That way, I have time to pull the cooled cookies from one pan before the next one comes out." The smile she shined on him was magnetic. "Coffee is all set for you. I turned it on when I heard the shower."

He chuckled and shook his head. Had someone, other than his parents, ever doted on him? That answer was no. It was a little weird to get used to.

He filled a cup of coffee, then glanced at Lara. "Do you want coffee?"

"Yes, please. Thank you."

He grinned as he poured them each a cup. She turned to take her cup from his hands; her cheeks were bright red. He cocked his head. "What's up?"

"I hope you won't mind that I rearranged some things in the cupboards. I have a system at home and at the bakery and..."

He laughed and kissed her forehead. "I don't mind. No one else will either. None of us cook, Lara. And by none of us, I really mean that. At home, we have a cook. She takes complete care of us and her daughter cleans and does laundry for us. We're built for what we do, not domestic things."

"Really? Your mom didn't cook?"

"I think she used to. But, when she and Dad married, he was already running GHOST and Mrs. James was in place. Mom is an operative as well, though not as active in the field, which created a ton of arguments between Mom and Dad. We used to listen to them argue about it when we were little."

"How many sisters and brothers do you have?"

"I have one brother and one sister. My brother's name is Matthew, and he's a year and a half younger. My sister's name is Kate, after my mom's best friend."

"Oh, that's awesome. I'll bet Kate was so honored when your parents named your sister after her."

He shrugged. "She was killed a long time ago. It's what brought my parents back together after a long time apart. I'm named after my mom's brother, who was my dad's best friend."

Lara stared at him for a long time. Her eyes teared up, and he leaned in and softly kissed her lips. "Hey. Don't cry."

"It's just so sweet. What an honor to be named after someone your parents loved."

He swallowed the emotion that welled up inside of him. It was an honor to be named after a loved one. He'd always known that. His parents told him often of his Uncle Tate and the fantastic man he was.

He kissed the top of Lara's head and turned when footsteps sounded on the stairs.

Maya entered the kitchen. "I smell cookies."

Tate laughed. "You do. Lara's been up for a while working."

Maya looked at Lara and smiled. "I love having you here." She stumbled to the coffeepot, then stopped at a plate of decorated cookies on the counter. She bit into one and moaned. "Mmm, this is soo good."

"Thank you."

He chuckled and kissed Lara on the lips then went to the plate of cookies before Maya ate them all up.

Lara walked around the center island and picked up a bag of frosting and began decorating the cooled cookies. He watched her for a while, both enthralled at the process and in admiration of her talent. He was losing his heart to Lara.

More footsteps came down the stairs and Tate grabbed another cookie before anyone else took one and Lara laughed. Maya watched him but made no comment. She had a way of watching people without emotion, which made her a fucking skilled operative. You never knew what she was thinking until she told you. Just like her mom.

Aidyn made his way to the kitchen. "I heard talking and smelled baking. How can a man sleep like that?"

Tate laughed. "You've slept through bombs in Afghanistan."

"Yeah, but I didn't smell the baking. Good thing the Taliban didn't cook."

They all laughed, and Tate's heart swelled. This was going to work out. His team was solid, they were going to get those BRR assholes to settle their shit and leave this town alone, and Lara... She fit in perfectly with the crew. She filled his heart with emotions he didn't know he lacked until he met her. She was perfect for him.

Lara made omelets for the four operatives here in the house, and as soon as Spencer and Adelaide walked in from their night shift, she had new ones made for them.

"Dammit, Lara. You're going to spoil us, and I'll kick anyone's ass who tries to stop it." Spencer boomed.

She laughed and began cleaning up the kitchen. Tate had said he'd be back in an hour to escort her to the bakery, and he did, thankfully, as long as the power was on she'd be safe, she wanted him there with her. Plus, they intended to install the generator on her building so she would always have power.

Her phone rang and she saw her father's name.

"Good morning, Dad."

"Good morning. Where are you? I'm at your house and you aren't here, and you weren't at the bakery this morning."

"I'm at a friend's."

"Shianne said you weren't with her."

She sighed and laid the dishrag on the edge of the

sink. She wasn't ready to tell him about Tate and her. "What do you need, Dad?"

He was quiet for a moment. "I wanted to make sure you're alright."

"You weren't worried last night."

"I was worried. I had to deal with your mother last night. She said you came over with a man and helped her back into bed."

"Yes. Tate came with me to help her."

"She's been having more issues than usual lately. I'm taking care of her, though, and we'll get it sorted."

"Has the doctor said anything specific?"

"No. Nothing different on that front."

"What's her diagnosis to begin with, Dad?"

"Lara. Your mom wants her privacy."

"How is telling your daughter what's wrong an invasion of privacy? I don't..."

"Lara. We've been over this. Over and over."

Lara closed her eyes and leaned against the counter. Her parents were so weird about her mom's illness. It often set her off on a tangent, which Shianne dutifully listened to, then changed the subject.

She took some deep breaths, then wearily said, "I have to go, Dad. I'll be at the bakery in a while."

"I'm on duty today, so I'll stop by."

"Okay." She ended the call, already feeling exhausted from dealing with her parents once again. They had so many secrets between them, and she wasn't privy to any of them. It was amazing in such a small town that anything could be a secret.

The back door opened, and Tate strode in. The concern on his face when he looked at her was clear.

"Hey, are you okay?"

She shook her head and chuckled. "I'm as good as I ever am dealing with my parents."

He kissed her forehead and shook his head. "I'm sorry. I don't know what to say other than I'm here if you need to talk about it."

"Thank you." She smiled. "Are you ready?"

"Yes. Just let me talk to Spencer for a moment."

She finished the kitchen clean-up and started dinner prep. Paxton's had delivered a large roast yesterday and she put that in a Crock Pot, added the seasonings, and set the timer on it. Wiping the counter down, she smiled when Tate came back into the room.

"All set?"

"Yes." She stepped into the dining room. "Hey guys, I have a roast in the Crock-Pot and the timer set. Supper will be ready around five."

Adelaide smiled. "Thanks, Lara."

Turning, she walked to the kitchen door and waited for Tate to grab another cookie. "I'm going to get fat with you living here."

"I know how we can work it off."

"That's what I'm talking about," he said as he took another bite of cookie. He made her heart feel light and happy and as if she could do anything. It was a wonderful feeling.

They stepped outside, and he pointed to the older Impala in the yard. "We're taking this. Until we can block the worm the BRR is using, we're not taking any chances."

"Sounds perfect."

As they drove to the bakery, Tate seemed pensive.

"Is everything alright?"

He turned and smiled at her. He moved his right hand

to lay on her left leg. "Yes. Can you tell me what you know of your father's relationship with the BRR? Any little conversation you can remember."

She looked at his profile for a long time as she tried remembering anything that would make sense.

"You know my relationship with my parents is weird, right? They've kept secrets forever. I've asked and I'm constantly shut down. Including this morning. I asked my father what the doctor said about my mom's condition, and he told me he didn't want to betray her privacy."

She pushed stray strands of hair from her cheek. "I'm family. I'd never betray her privacy and letting me in shouldn't be considered a betrayal, either. I'm their daughter."

She took a deep breath and let it out slowly to stop the emotions she always summoned when she thought about this or talked about it. She swallowed to moisten her throat, then shrugged. "I'm as much of an outsider as you are where that's concerned."

"So you don't know if your father has ever spent any time with Everett Howard or Craig Howard or any of the BRR Council?"

"Maybe. As a liaison with the mayor. Maybe in the past on issues with theft. In years past, things weren't as tense as they are now. They would come down to trade and sometimes when trading didn't get them what they wanted, they'd break in and steal things. Usually, it was gas. Between Paxton's Grocery Store and a few of the other trades they made in the area, they managed enough sugar. They found enough of the other products they needed and then mostly, the rest of the year, we seldom saw or heard them. There was a pattern. They'd come down the first week of the month to trade and then go back up. There weren't only two or three of them who came down and there wasn't any trouble."

"So this is the first year trading has stopped?"

"No. Last year. The mayor was newly elected, and he ran on the platform of reform. The elixir hurt a bunch of kids last year. It was too strong and two of them died; three or four of them have long-lasting health issues. Lung issues and one of them has heart issues now. The mayor thinks they laced the elixir with something on purpose to destroy us."

"What do you think?"

"Why would they do that? It had been peaceful. They'd know it would cause a war. It makes no sense. Then the mayor brokered the deal to have Fort Abraham built here, and that stirred things up more. But, to be honest, I think that's more Craig Howard's dealings than anything."

He glanced at her, then turned to the road once more. "Because Craig will be president one day?"

"Yeah. They posture when they know they'll be in charge. They're all going to make changes, make life better, on and on. Just like our elections down here, except they don't have elections."

THIRTY-SEVEN

Tate entered the bakery first. "Stay behind me." He whispered. His weapon raised before him, he crouched, ready to pounce if need be.

"Okay."

He listened and tiptoed through the back hallway to the kitchen. No one lurked inside the kitchen, and they crept to the utility room. Using his toe, he pushed the door open and looked inside. The bathroom was next to that and was equally small and empty.

The next room was her little office, which took little time to clear. He led them into the front of the bakery. Nothing seemed out of place. Lara took a deep breath and relaxed her shoulders.

He nodded, then kissed her lips. "All clear."

"Thank you." She made her way to the coffeemaker and turned it on. "I'll have coffee ready in a minute."

"I can't stay, baby. I'm headed back to work. At four, I'll be here to bring you home. If you need anything in the meantime, call me. Spencer and Henry will be here in an hour to install the generator."

She rounded the counter to turn on the register and gasped.

He was there in an instant. He gently took the note from her trembling fingers.

The note was short and to the point. "Fuck you."

He walked to the front door and pulled it open. It was unlocked.

"We locked that last night when we left here."

"I know."

Tate looked at the lock and saw some scratches on the front where they'd used something other than a key to open it.

Pulling his phone from his pocket, he called the sheriff.

"Good morning, Mr. Vickers. What can I do for you today?"

"Lara Bennit's bakery was broken into again yesterday."

"Are you shitting me? Is it busted up again?"

"No. They picked the lock and left a note on her register."

He heard the sheriff's chair squeak as he leaned back into it. "I'll be right out there. Have you called Keaton?"

"And what would that do, exactly?"

The sheriff muttered something under his breath and the line went dead. Tate turned to her and saw how pale she was. He went to her and pulled her in close for a hug.

"I'll do everything I can to keep you safe."

Her shaking arms wrapped around his waist. "I know."

Still holding his phone, he stepped back and smiled at her. "Let's sit down a minute."

He led her to the little table in front of the window

and sat across from her. He held her hand on top of the table and dialed his dad.

Tapping the speaker icon, he laid his phone on the table and pointed to his dad's name. Her eyes rounded and he smiled.

"Hey, Tate. How are things going?"

"Hey, Dad. First, you're on speaker. I'm here with Lara Bennit. Lara is the best cookie baker in the world and owns Lara's Delights."

"It's nice to meet you, Lara. My name is Gaige Vickers."

"Hi, Mr. Vickers. It's nice to meet you too."

A voice in the background could be heard. "Is that Tate? Tate, honey, how are you?"

Tate chuckled and looked at Lara. "Lara, meet my mom, Sophie Vickers."

"Hello, Mrs. Vickers."

"Please call me Sophie. Tate, how are you getting on there in Glen Hollow? We've been reading the reports."

He smiled at Lara and felt his cheeks heat.

"We're getting along alright. Still working on the BRR issue. That's why I'm calling. The BRR has targeted Lara. They have broken into her bakery four times in the last month. The last time was last night. No damage, except maybe the lock. I'm wondering if you can spare a couple of operatives to come down here and help us with additional security until we can get things settled."

"I think we can manage that. I know any one of them would gladly come down to see their kid. What are you up against, so I know who to send?"

"Mostly, and this is sensitive, Lara's father is a sheriff's deputy here. But he's gone soft on the BRR. As in, there's something weird going on with him and them.

Lara doesn't know what it is, and we haven't figured it out yet. We'll install a generator here in the bakery today. That should keep her security intact. But I'd like someone here with her during the day. She's with me at night. And Spencer is slightly impaired with his foot until he heals."

He watched Lara's cheeks turn a beautiful shade of red. He brushed the back of his forefinger down her heated cheek and winked at her.

His mom spoke so fast it made him laugh. "I'll come down there."

His parents whispered to each other, and he grinned at Lara as they listened, but couldn't hear anything specific.

"How about your mom and me? Will we do?"

"Yes. We'd love that."

"What do you need us to bring?"

"More security cameras. A few generators. And, can you see if RAPTOR's cyber unit has some crack software for us to ferret out a worm the BRR installed in business point-of-sale and messaging software? We'd like to kill that worm."

"Okay. We'll see what we can gather. We'll be down there tonight."

"Thanks, Dad. Love you, Mom."

"I love you too, Tate."

His parents whispered again, and he ended the call just as Lara was about to say goodbye. "They wouldn't hear you, baby. Mom's got her mind made up, and I'd bet my dad is ambivalent about coming down here."

"Why?"

"Because this is my operation. He's always been that way. He lets me do what I need to do. I always know he's there for me. It's how I became the man I am."

She stood and sat on his lap. "I love the man you are."

Her lips touched his instantly and while he enjoyed kissing her, she'd just said she loved him. Well, she said she loved the man he is. Did that mean him? Does she love him? Was he supposed to say it back? Was this getting murky?

THIRTY-EIGHT

She meant to say he was a great man. They'd molded a great man, and she loved that. She did. But it was too soon to know if she loved Tate. Wasn't it? So much had gone on she didn't even know what today was, let alone if she loved someone.

She pulled away from his lips when she heard her phone ring and stood from his lap.

"This is Lara."

"Hey, is Shianne, are you open today?"

"Yes. I'm open. I just got here and have nothing fresh baked yet."

"Okay. Can I stop in? I want to show you my dress for the ball."

"Sure."

She pocketed her phone. "Shianne is on her way over."

"I'm sorry I can't stay with you today, Lara. Are you sure you'll be alright here? I can take you home."

"Tate. I can't keep pulling you away from work. As much as I love spending time with you, I feel terribly guilty. And now your parents are coming to town. Where will they sleep?"

He grinned. "I thought you and I would go to your place, and they can have my room."

She smiled and felt the heat crawl up her body. "I'd like that. That way, we don't have to be so quiet."

It was his turn to go pink, but he stalked to her and pulled her tightly to his body. His lips landed against hers and his tongue dove into her mouth. Their tongues danced together, and she felt him grow rigid. It was exciting how his body reacted to hers. His hands cupped her face on either side, and he tilted her head slightly before dominating her mouth once more.

"Oh, my god. Right here in front of everyone."

She jumped back as Shianne grinned like the Grinch. But when Tate spoke, her grin turned into an open-mouthed gape.

"I'll kiss her in front of anyone who's around. I happen to like kissing her."

Shianne closed her mouth, then looked into her eyes. Her cheeks turned bright red and for the first time in a long time, Shianne was speechless.

"Okay," she squeaked out.

Lara laughed. She stood on her toes and kissed Tate quickly. "Thank you for bringing me to work."

"Call me if you have any trouble."

"I will."

He swatted her on the ass, nodded to Shianne, and walked out the back door.

Shianne looked at her, and Lara laughed. "We're together."

"Well, duh!"

"His parents are coming into town tonight, too."

"What for? Is it to meet you? Oh my god, what on earth has happened in just a few days? You have a lot to tell me."

Lara laughed and sauntered to the coffeemaker and poured them each a cup.

Shianne hung her dress bag on the door to the office and came back for her cup of coffee.

They sat at the table she and Tate had just vacated and she told Shianne all about Kent, the power outages, and Tate's parents.

"Basically, I'm interrupting his job. My dad is too by not doing his job and Tate called in support. As soon as his mom found out about me, she jumped at the chance to come down here. Plus, I'm sure they miss him, so they'll be here tonight."

"Wow." Shianne sipped her coffee and stared.

"Is your store open today?"

"Yes. The power is back on and I've dragged my manual credit card system from the basement so I can still sell clothing and accessories if the power goes out again. I have a money bag with change and we're going old school."

Lara laughed. "Awesome. Let's see the dress."

Shianne set her coffee on the counter and unzipped the dress bag. She pulled her dress free with a flourish.

"Oh, Shi, it's gorgeous."

It was, too. A dark gray, one-shouldered, beaded bodice dress with a full skirt. And with her coloring, her dark hair and creamy skin, she would be the belle of the ball.

Shianne pulled the dress from the door and held it before her. She twirled around just as Spencer limped through the front door.

He gawked, while Shianne's cheeks turned a beautiful pink.

Lara grinned. "That's her dress for the Ball. Isn't it gorgeous?"

Spencer nodded. He shuffled his feet, then said, "Ah. Yes. Gorgeous."

He shook the stunned look from his face and said, "I brought the generator. I need access to the basement, and can you show me your power panel?"

"Sure." She glanced at Shianne and escorted him to the back door. Next to the back door was an alcove. Inside was the door to the basement.

She stopped before going down the steps. "Can you do this?"

"Yeah. It's not graceful, but I can manage. Henry will do all the heavy lifting though."

She led the way downstairs, flipping lights on as she went, then pointed to the far wall. "That's the power panel there."

He managed the stairs by using the railings on either side and lifting his body down. "Perfect. It'll take me about an hour."

"I'll be upstairs if you need anything."

She ascended the stairs and found Shianne zipping her dress into the bag, her cheeks still bright pink.

"I've hardly said two words to him since we made this date, and I don't know what to say."

Lara laughed. "You are never one to not know what to say. What would you say to anyone else?"

She put her hand on her hip. "Hey, what do you think of those BRR bastards?"

"Well, since they're battling them, that would work."

Shianne blew out a big breath and moved her bangs off her face.

"I'm worrying about nothing. I'll get back to work and see you later. What time are Tate's parents arriving?"

"I don't know. He mentioned that it's about a four-hour drive. So, if they leave by noon, they'll be here at four."

"Where are they staying?"

"At the house. Tate's coming to my house."

"No way!" Shianne hugged her. "You still didn't tell me all about it."

"I'm not going to. Suffice it to say, it's personal. And, it's too new."

THIRTY-NINE

Tate called the sheriff as he drove to the base.

"Twice in a morning, Mr. Vickers."

"Yes. I'd like to set up a meeting with the president of the BRR, yourself, and the mayor. Do you have a way to do that?"

"Why do you want to do that?"

"Look, we can play these tit-for-tat games all day long, but it gets us nowhere. Sitting down and having a dialog with them seems to be the way to go. No one has to be a go-between and it seems the most expeditious way to get this all done."

"If they were reasonable, sure. However, these are not reasonable people. They've lived up on the mountain for over sixty years. They have their own set of laws and their own values. None of which are our laws or values."

"What does it hurt to try?"

"It gives them the power to say no. It makes them think they have the upper hand. I know you're new to town, but these animals don't think the way we do."

"So, you won't help me?"

"No, Mr. Vickers, I won't help you."

The call ended and Tate was more irritated than he'd been before. By the time he arrived at the construction site, he was in a mood. A dark mood.

He stalked into the construction trailer and noted Aidyn wasn't around. He poured a cup of coffee and as he lifted it to his lips, the sharp odor of construction coffee, as they'd coined it, made his stomach lurch.

Setting the cup aside, he pulled his phone out and called Aidyn.

"Hey, are you back?"

"Yeah. Where are you?"

"I'm out back where we saw those BRR kids the other day. Come on back here so I can show you what I've found."

Tate stalked out the door and strode across the construction site. Workers were in the basement of the main building working. Some waved as he passed, others were hauling or working and didn't notice him.

He found Aidyn near the fence, kicking at the ground.

"What have you found?"

Aidyn pointed up to the tree on the outside of the fence.

"If you look up there, you'll see wires." He walked a few steps to the fence where it had been cut then re-hooked together.

"Right here is where they entered the grounds." He moved a few feet over to the pipe they'd broken, which had since been repaired.

"So we figured out they'd patched into the base's power; here's where they did it."

Tate looked at the ground where Aidyn pointed with his toe. "They patched into the power not by cutting the wires—that was a distraction. They ran a wire through a separate pipe."

Aidyn dug with his fingers. The loose dirt moved easily as he uncovered a smaller white PVC pipe laid in the ground. He pushed the dirt away from the end of it and fully exposed the pipe with wires protruding from it.

"We saw that smaller pipe yesterday when we assessed the damage. That skinny guy helping the electrician told me it was nothing connected to the BRR damage." Aidyn looked him in the eye. "What do you make of that?"

Tate looked toward the basement where the workers assembled. "I think we have someone who either doesn't know what he's doing or is involved with the BRR."

"That's what I thought at first too." He walked down the fence line a few feet. He squeezed between the fence and the storage containers which were being lined up along the fence to secure the area. "Then I saw this." He bent and tugged on a wire laying in the brush, partially covered with leaves and weeds. "This wire is connected to the large generator that supplies the base. I think they've patched in, just in case they lose power from their own worm."

"Well, I hate to give them credit, but that's fucking clever."

"It sure is."

"So, why fuck with the town's power? Why mess with the local businesses?"

Aidyn shrugged. "I only have theories. They're mad at businesses for not trading with them, number one. A second is they're testing the power scramblers and whether it interrupts their power. And third. And this is far-reaching, but they just like keeping the townies on their toes. A sort of terrorism, never knowing what or when something will happen."

Tate nodded. "Then why Lara? When I took her in today, there was a note on her register that said, 'Fuck You'. They'd come in through the front door by picking the lock."

Aidyn straightened his shoulders. "There's still something fishy with Keaton and the BRR. Kent is obviously mad at Keaton and targeting Lara. It's more than Lara deciding not to trade with them. There are other businesses that have refused to trade with them who haven't been targeted."

"Or, my theory is Kent is Keaton's son."

Aidyn stared at him for a few moments then nodded. "Same eyes."

Tate nodded. That was the déjà vu he'd felt. He rubbed his forehead. "I don't know why I didn't put that together, I just had this hunch."

"You're too close to it."

Tate's heart raced. He took deep breaths to settle it down and get his emotions under control. He'd chided himself when Spencer got hurt that he'd focused too much on Lara. He was doing it again.

"Right." Tate looked at the wire and the dirt where it had been disrupted and then put it back and stamped down. "My parents are coming today and bringing more cameras and software we can use to kill the worm the BRR installed in apps."

He looked at the construction crew in the basement of the main building, installing the elevator shaft. "Someone knows they've patched into the electrical system and agreed to seal it up saying nothing. The pipe was repaired, and the wires quietly connected."

Tate rubbed the back of his neck with his fingers. "Yep. But, it's easy for the BRR to find people and get them to help. They watch everything that goes on down here. Blackmail can turn the strongest of allies." He looked at Aidyn. "Great job, Aidyn. You've done a fantastic job out here."

"Thanks. What are our next steps?"

Tate glanced around and weighed the advantages and disadvantages against turning in one of the crew. At this point, it didn't matter. There'd be another person taking their place sooner rather than later.

FORTY

Lara spent the day baking. Business was slower today than it had been. The people in town had done their best by helping her out of a tough spot, but they'd gone on to their daily lives now.

It gave her time to catch up. Spencer and Henry had finished with the generator and her doorbell now rang again. It comforted her that no one would sneak in. Plus, Tate insisted she carry, so she had her trusty sidekick with her.

She decorated her second batch of cookies for home tonight. She'd made the operatives at Tate's a batch of cookies because they seemed to like them. These were cute. She'd made guns, targets, handcuffs, and computers out of round cookies. It was a great exercise in her art skills.

For her house tonight and Tate's parents, she made a goldenrod flower, which was Kentucky's state flower. A cardinal on a white cookie, which was their state bird and cookies with all of their names on them in different colors.

She had fresh bread in the oven right now, which would come out soon, and she'd pull together a nice supper for them tonight. And Paxton's was due to deliver groceries soon.

The doorbell sounded, and she set her frosting tube on the counter and pulled a towel from the edge of the sink. Wiping her hands as she walked out to the bakery, she froze when she saw an older lady standing in the middle of the room. Her clothing spoke of the women up on the hill; flour-sack dresses were common up there. They made most of their own clothes and weren't up on the latest fashion trends.

"May I help you?" Lara asked tentatively. She walked behind the counter, feeling safer keeping the counter between them.

The woman was older, maybe about her mother's age. She seemed nervous and her eyes roamed around the room, taking everything in. Her graying hair was tied back into a bun. Lara allowed her the time she needed, or wanted, and focused on looking confident.

"I came down to warn you, miss. Please." Her bottom lip shook. "Please tell your father to honor his word."

"I don't understand. What word? What did he promise?"

The woman backed toward the door, her face a mask of forced pleasantry. "Please. Tell him."

The woman slipped through the open door and disappeared. Lara rushed to the front of the bakery and scoured the parking lot, but the woman had gone.

The oven timer sounded, yet Lara hesitated. She scanned up and down the road to see if the woman might drive by; she saw no one. It was eerily quiet outside.

She locked the door and turned the sign for her lunch

hour and hurried to the kitchen to pull her bread from the oven. Her hands shook as she set the loaves on the stove to cool. Laying her hot pads alongside, she clasped her hands together and took some deep breaths. To her knowledge, no one from Hickory Hills had ever come down here into her bakery. Now it had been twice in a week.

She pulled her phone out and dialed her dad. The phone went instantly to voicemail. She didn't leave one. Frankly, she didn't want to give him a heads-up and time to think of a lie. She shook her head and pocketed her phone.

A knock on her back door made her jump and squeak. She took a deep breath to get herself under control. Padding to the back door, afraid to make a sound, she pressed her ear to the door at the same time the knocking sounded again and she jumped.

Her voice shook. "Yes."

"It's Alan with Paxton's Grocery with your order, Lara."

She managed to unlock the door, though it was a struggle, the way she shook. The young man holding the crates with her groceries smiled at her. "I didn't mean to scare you."

"No. No." She took a deep breath. "It's fine. My imagination has gotten the better of me today."

He shook his head, and she stepped back to open the door for him. He walked to the kitchen and set her groceries on the table, then pulled his notepad from his inside pocket with an invoice for her to sign.

She scribbled her signature and handed him back his notepad. "What happened to the electronic pads you had?"

"The power outages created too many issues for us. So, we're back to pen and paper until we can count on it again."

"Yes, we're all struggling these days."

"Have a great day, Lara."

He strode out of her kitchen and she followed him to the back door and locked herself inside once again. Taking in deep breaths, she forced herself to be brave and keep on moving through her day. She had a meal to prepare for her boyfriend's parents. At least, she assumed Tate was her boyfriend. They hadn't had that conversation. Was that even a conversation adults had? They were having sex. She would not call herself his sex buddy. Certainly not to his parents. She was still old-fashioned enough that she only dated one man at a time. She didn't sleep around, and she definitely wouldn't date someone else while she was having sex with Tate. She didn't know how he felt about that though.

Taking a deep breath, she moved her freshly frosted cookies to a side counter and turned the little fan on to speed the drying of her frosting. She unpacked her groceries and set aside the brisket for dinner tonight. Pulling her Instant Pot from the shelf, she began preparing dinner for tonight and set aside thoughts of how Tate felt about her and their relationship. They'd have the chat soon enough. She knew right now he was working hard.

FORTY-ONE

Tate knocked on the back door and called out. "Tara, it's me."

He listened, then heard her footsteps approach and the locks twist on the door. When she opened the door, she stepped back, and he saw the worry on her face.

"Hey. Are you okay?"

She nodded but didn't make eye contact, and his stomach dipped while he stepped inside and closed the door. Turning the locks, he faced her and saw the hard set of her mouth.

"Tell me what's happened."

"I've been—it's stupid. I worked myself up. It's all so immature. I don't even know what to say."

He shook his head and pulled her to his chest. He wrapped his arms around her and held her close. "You sure feel good against me, baby."

She sobbed, and he squeezed her closer. "You smell good. Cookies and bread and all things delicious. I can't wait to introduce you to my parents. They've waited forever for me to meet someone special."

She mumbled into his chest. "I'm special?"

He chuckled. "Of course, you are. How can you not know that?"

She lifted her head and wiped her eyes. Stepping back, she sniffed and let out a long breath.

"I've been driving myself crazy with all the things. I'm meeting your parents, but I didn't know if I'm actually considered your girlfriend. I didn't know if adults still talked about being boyfriend and girlfriend and I worried I looked too old-fashioned. But, I am old-fashioned. Sort of. I mean, we've had sex, so that's not old-fashioned. But, you are...there's something special about you, Tate. I've thrown away many of my reservations because you are... I feel different about you." She swiped at her face once more and dried her fingers on her thighs. "Ugh. I'm sorry. It's just been a lot lately and I'm overreacting and making things much bigger than they need to be and then that lady came in here and I just got all...weird."

"What lady?"

"The one from the hill." She sniffed lightly again, and his heartbeat raced.

"The hill? As in Hickory Hills? Someone came in here from up there?"

She froze as her eyes searched his face. "Yeah."

"What did she want?"

Lara wiped under her eyes again and blew out a breath. "She had a message for my dad."

"What message?"

She cleared her throat lightly. "Um. She said he should honor his word."

"What word?"

"She wouldn't say."

"Did you call your dad?"

"I tried. But his phone went directly to voicemail. I didn't leave a message. Then I had a grocery delivery and my mind started racing and I just..." She shrugged. "I'm sorry. I promise you I'm not a nutcase. I've never dealt with this much stress, and I guess I'm not handling it well."

He took her hand and led her to the kitchen. He pulled the stools tucked under her table out and motioned for her to sit down. Then he took the stool next to her, but turned to face her. Pulling her hands into his, his eyes locked on hers.

"All those things you tried to say about me before. Special or different. I feel that for you, Lara. No one has ever been as special as you. I've given this a lot of thought, too. My heart calls out to you. My body responds to you. Not just," he motioned toward his lower area. "Here. It obviously responds to you there. But, here." He put her hand on his heart. "My heart gets excited when it sees you."

He moved their hands to his chest. "And here. My breathing gets weird and sputters when you're near." He moved their hands to his head. "And, here. My brain is constantly thinking of you."

"Tate." Her voice was soft.

"I'm sorry we haven't had this conversation before this. It seems like there's always something going on or someone is around. And it's a hard discussion to have because I didn't want to chase you away."

She burst out laughing. "Oh, my god. Tate. I couldn't run from you. Ever."

He wrapped his arms around her waist and pulled her

to him. She situated herself on his lap, her legs wrapped around his waist, her arms wrapped around his shoulders.

"I love you, Lara Bennit. You surprised me this morning. But, I've thought about what it means to love someone and everything I feel for you tells me I love you. I've never been in love before, so it took me a minute to understand my feelings."

She looked into his eyes. The blue of hers was beautiful and true and mesmerizing. "I love you, Tate Vickers."

Her lips touched his softly. Their kiss was a promise to each other. It was a promise he intended to keep. His arms slid up her back and he enjoyed the feel of her body pressed to his. Her legs wrapped around his waist made him think of other carnal thoughts and he thought with the doors locked, they could have sex here. It'd be one of the many places they would make love.

He pulled her blouse from the back of her slacks and his hands roamed up her naked back, the feel of her heated skin a balm to his fingers. She wriggled on his lap and he groaned.

"I'm going to have you right here, Lara."

"Yes," she whispered in his ear. Her tongue then circled the shell of his ear and he groaned again.

He reached around and slipped his fingers under her bra, squeezed her breast and made her breathing hitch.

Lara unbuttoned the front of her blouse and the instant she pulled it open, his mouth was on her breast. He suckled her into his mouth, and she rotated her hips to grind against his rapidly thickening cock.

The ringing of his phone was easy to ignore. At first. Her hips ground against him again and he put his hands on either side of her hips and ground her harder onto him. She gasped, and he intended to do it again when she stopped moving.

"Are you on duty? Do you have to answer?"

"Fuck."

She giggled and pulled from him, then stood as he reached back and pulled his phone from his pocket. "Yeah."

"Hey, are we interrupting something?" His mom asked.

"No, Mom. It's good."

Lara smiled at him, and he watched sadly as she buttoned her blouse and his boner quickly died as he listened to his mom.

"We're only about fifteen minutes from Glen Hollow. Where should we meet you?"

He gave them directions to the bakery and pocketed his phone. "They're almost here."

"What do you think of your parents staying in my spare bedroom? I know they can stay in your room at the house, but it'll be more private at my house, and you can spend more time with them. And so can I."

"Are you sure?"

"I am." She smiled at him and his heart swelled.

FORTY-TWO

Lara stood next to the counter in the bakery as Tate opened the front door for his parents.

His mom ran up to him first and hugged him for a long time. He looked like her. Dark hair, dark eyes, beautiful. His dad entered next. That's where he got his height from. And his build. They were both broad shouldered, muscular, and confident. Tate hugged his dad, then turned to her.

"Mom and Dad, this is Lara. Lara, my parents, Sophie and Gaige Vickers."

She walked forward, and Sophie hugged her warmly. "It's nice to meet you," Sophie whispered in her ear.

"It's nice to meet you too."

Gaige hugged her next. It was a friendly hug, firm and welcoming. He stood back and met her gaze. "We're happy to meet you, Lara."

"I'm happy to meet you, too."

She stepped back and Tate wrapped his arm around her.

Sophie looked around. "Lara, this is a lovely bakery."

"Thank you. Would you like the tour? It won't take long." She laughed and Sophie smiled.

"I'd love a tour."

Lara held her hand out to the tables. "My friend and I painted the tables. My dad had the glass tops made for them. I fill the cases every morning. Coffee is made fresh each day, several times a day. This town has been very good to me. I'm busy most days."

She led them into the kitchen, and Sophie inhaled. "Oh, wow. This room smells heavenly."

Lara smiled, and her cheeks heated. "Thank you. I put in extra effort today to welcome you. Fresh bread, beef brisket in the Instant Pot, and cookies baked just for you and the team members at the house. They seem to like them, too."

Sophie looked at the cookies. "You're an artist."

She shrugged. Tate stepped forward. "Wait till you taste them." He picked one off the plate, and she giggled.

Sophie exclaimed. "Tate. They were arranged so nicely."

"Mom. Seriously, they are so good," he said with his mouth full.

Gaige picked one off the plate, bit into it and moaned. "He's right."

Sophie leaned forward and took a cookie with her name on it. She took a quick bite, closed her eyes and hummed her appreciation. Lara's heart felt ready to burst. Her mom had never eaten her cookies. She said she didn't want the sugar.

The timer on the Instant Pot dinged, and Lara picked up a wooden spoon. She used the spoon to move the pressured top and release the steam. The room filled with the additional aroma of beef brisket. She felt proud at the impression she'd made so far.

Her phone rang, and she laid the spoon down and glanced at her phone. She looked at Tate. "My dad."

He nodded and ushered his parents into the bakery, and she answered her phone.

"Hi, Dad."

"Hey, Lara. Did you try calling me earlier?"

"Yes. An older woman from Hickory Hills came into the bakery today and gave me a message to share with you. She said, 'Tell your father to honor his word. Please.' What does that mean?"

"What did she look like?"

"She was older, with gray hair. What does it mean?"

Her dad avoided answering the question. She pressed. "Dad…"

Tate came back into the kitchen and stood next to her. She tapped the speaker on her phone, listening in the silence for some kind of response.

"Dad. Why aren't you answering me?"

"It's hard to answer when I don't know who it was."

"Really? Because there are a lot of women up on the mountain who want you to honor your word?"

"What are you insinuating?"

"I'm insinuating that you're involved in some way with the BRR and it has drawn me into it. I'm sick of being used to get back at you. Whatever is going on up there. With you. You must end it."

"You don't know what you're asking of me."

"What did you get yourself involved in?"

"I have to go, Lara."

The line went dead and she pocketed her phone. Tate's jaw clenched as he looked into her eyes.

Lara sighed. "I can't imagine what he's involved in."

"I can't either." He kissed her forehead. "You've delivered your message, and he knows you suspect something. Let's go home and eat and ignore this for a while. I have to go back out tonight, and I'll see if I can find out more about what's happening up there."

"Okay."

She wrapped her arms around his waist, looking for a comfort only he could provide; he wrapped her in his warm, powerful arms.

"I made that plate of cookies for your teammates. Can we run them by on our way to my place?"

"Sure."

She pulled the groceries from the refrigerator and repacked them in the crate Paxton's had left. Then Tate grabbed the Instant Pot and called to his parents.

Sophie and Gaige came back and helped them carry food items to the car. Sophie laughed. "Nice ride. That was great to think about the older vehicles."

"Yeah. It's working for us for the time being. Baxter at the construction site has been cool as well."

Once they had loaded the vehicle, Lara locked up the bakery, Gaige and Sophie climbed in the back seat, and Tate drove them around the front to get into their vehicle.

Just as they turned onto the road, the Jeep from the hill, with Kent driving, barreled past them and sped off down the road.

"Was he watching?"

Tate shook his head. "I didn't see him anywhere. Unless he was hiding somewhere."

"It's creepy that he can watch unnoticed."

He leaned over and touched her face with his fingers. "I know. Remember to be careful when you're here."

"I will."

"I plan on getting this under control soon."

She laid her hand against his. "I know you will."

FORTY-THREE

Lan gave the Tates' parents a tour of her home and Sophie was in the spare bedroom settling in. Gage sat in the living room on his computer while she gathered plates and silverware and set the table.

The brisket was still in the Instant Pot and hot, so she pulled it from inside and set it on a platter. She'd made broccoli and carrots to go with it and those were on the stove staying in the pan.

The juices left in the Instant Pot were still hot and she carried it to the back door and slipped outside to dump it in the garbage can before the fats inside congealed and she'd have to scrape it out. Her garbage can was behind her garage on a cement pad, where she didn't have to look at it from the house.

Setting the pot on the cement pad, she lifted the lid on her garbage can then moved a paper bag she'd thrown away yesterday to the top and opened it up. She lifted the pot and poured the hot liquid into the bag.

Setting it down again, she rolled the bag closed and closed the lid.

As she headed back to the house, a cloth covered her head. She swung the pot but failed to connect to anyone. It clattered to the ground. A gigantic hand covered her mouth. She was lifted, kicking and screaming, and carried to a vehicle. She stiffened so they couldn't put her inside. They punched her in the stomach, and she doubled over. They tossed her inside. Something wet covered her mouth and nose and she lost consciousness.

———

Lara sat tied in a chair, the bag or hood still over her head. She could hear someone walking around on a wooden floor, so she assumed she was in a house. She didn't remember the drive to wherever she was.

A door creaked and heavier footsteps entered the house. They stopped in front of her. She held her breath but didn't move or say anything. The footsteps moved away from her and she let her breathing continue. She could see some shadows as they moved past a window. The light footsteps were of a woman based on the flowing dress as she moved.

"She say anything?"

"No, sir."

"Good. Say nothing to her."

"Yes, sir."

"Have her readied for the wedding at six tonight. We'll wed as the sun begins to set."

"Yes, sir."

The heavy footsteps passed by her without stopping and her heartbeat raced as the words whirred through her head. Wedding. We'll wed. He couldn't mean he was to marry her. She wouldn't do it. She wouldn't say vows to another man. Certainly not someone she didn't know.

She swallowed and tried taking steady breaths. Her stomach roiled, and she worried she'd vomit. How many times today had she felt that way?

The woman shuffled toward her and stopped in front of her. Her voice was soft when she said, "I'm taking the hood off now."

Her hands were gentle as she lifted the hood from the bottom and held it away from her nose and mouth as she gently lifted it from her head.

"It'll be easier to breathe now."

She shuffled over to the counter where she'd been working and brought over a pestle and mortar and looked at her face. "The ether gave you a tiny rash. I'll put the poultice of aloe vera and oatmeal on to help you heal. I've added a bit of honey to make it stick."

She dipped her finger into the bowl and scooped out a small amount of the poultice. Moving toward Lara, she winced. "It won't hurt. I've used this on my children."

Lara looked into her eyes. They were old eyes, faded blue. The lines around her eyes and mouth spoke of age, of a woman who'd lived a hard life and had seen her better years pass by. Lara guessed her to be in her seventies.

"Why am I here?"

"You heard Everett. He's marrying you tonight."

"No. I won't marry him."

The older woman grinned. "You will."

"No, I won't."

The woman stopped spreading the poultice on her

face and grinned at her. "If you don't marry Everett, he'll kill your man."

"My man." Her breathing quickened. "You mean Tate?"

The older woman nodded.

"But why?"

The woman chuckled. "I'm afraid you've been caught up in the dirty deeds of your father. Everett believes if you're his wife, your father will have no choice but to honor his word and help us."

"But I have nothing to do with that."

"That's right. And unfortunate." She dabbed the rest of the poultice around her mouth.

The door opened again, and Kent walked into the cabin. He stared at her for a long time, but she remained steady. She stared at him in return and refused to look scared. Inside though, she'd never been more scared in her life.

Kent played with something in his hand, and she saw it was her phone. He twirled it around in his hands as he grinned.

"So, Lara, the owner of the bakery. Lara Bennit." He practically spat her last name.

"And you're Kent. Kent of the hooligans who damaged my bakery."

"Your smart mouth is going to learn the rules here very soon."

She stared into his eyes, and he shrugged then rubbed his temples. He looked just like her dad when he did that. That almost stopped her breathing. She stared at him intently and noticed things about him. His eyes were the same blue. His hairline had that same peak at the temples as her father. Then he chuckled and she knew.

She swallowed and Kent tapped on her phone. He tapped her phone again and she could hear it ringing on the other end.

"Your father is going to want to know where you are. You tell him he needs to come and get you before six tonight or he'll find you a married woman."

The phone rang again and finally her father answered. "Lara, honey, I don't have time right now I have to..."

"Dad. I've been kidnapped. The BRR have me. I'm here with Kent right now."

Kent laughed. "Hello, Keaton. Or should I say Dad?"

Her father sputtered on the other end of the phone. Finally, he said, "Kent. Don't do this."

"We've told you over and over you need to honor your word. To date you've failed to distribute our elixir to other towns. You've failed to get the council to reinstate the deferment."

"Lara has nothing to do with this."

"She'll be paying the price for you. At six o'clock tonight, if you haven't come up here and gotten your first batch of elixir for distribution, Lara will be getting married to Everett."

"No. Please don't do that to her. She has nothing to do with this."

"Look. Dad. You made promises. You've not kept any of them."

"Lara, honey, I'll do anything to help you...Everything to help you. I promise."

"Warn Tate. They've threatened him."

Kent tapped the end call icon and the call disconnected.

FORTY-FOUR

"Lara!" He called out the door. Looking across the yard near the garage, he saw something silver laying on the ground near the garbage cans. His stomach rolled as he neared it and saw her Instant Pot. It looked as though it had been kicked over or dropped. Lifting the lid to the can, he looked inside and saw the juice from the brisket. His gut seized.

His dad approached. "Anything?"

"No." He pointed at the Instant Pot. "She came out here to dump the grease." His voice caught. "They took her, Dad."

"Call Keaton. I'll call your teammates."

Tate called Keaton Bennit. It rang more than a few times and his anger boiled.

"Tate. They…"

"Where is she?"

"Kent has her."

"Why?"

"Because of me."

"What did you do?"

He heard Keaton inhale a deep breath, then his voice shook when he responded. "I promised to distribute their elixir to help raise the money to pay the taxes."

"You what?" Tate swiped his hand down his face. "Why the fuck would you agree to that?"

"They were blackmailing me."

"For what?"

Keaton didn't answer and he lost any shred of patience he had left.

"Keaton, dammit, I swear to God if they harm her, I will do everything in my power to bring you down."

"We have to get her before six tonight. Everett is threatening to marry her at six. To make her pay for my misdeeds."

Tate pulled the phone from his ear and looked up the mountain. Gaige took his phone gently and finished speaking to Keaton.

Tears filled his eyes as he thought of her up there, scared and alone. He'd promised her he'd keep her safe. He'd broken his promise.

He half listened to his dad talk to that piece-of-shit deputy but he couldn't catch his breath. He'd just found her and now...

His dad pulled him in for a hug and whispered, "We'll get her back. Let's go, your teammates are ready to help you find her."

He reluctantly followed his dad inside. He wanted to run up that mountain right. The. Fuck. Now.

———

TATE BUCKLED his tactical belt around his waist and stood.

His mom stared into his eyes. "Okay. Please be careful."

He nodded and kissed her temple, then slipped out the back door. He looked around for anyone watching. He'd scoured Lara's cameras earlier and saw them take her. He nearly vomited when he watched her struggle while he was in the house on his computer. She meant more to him than anything, including this mission, if he were being honest.

His parents followed him out, driving in their vehicle to the GHOST house.

He jumped in the old Malibu and called Aidyn.

"Yeah."

"I'm on my way."

"We're ready."

He hung up and navigated a corner to drive past the bakery on the off chance they took her there. No signs of anyone on the property.

As he pulled into the driveway of the GHOST house, his heart raced. He swallowed then opened his door just as his dad reached him.

"Tate. Son. I know what you're feeling right now. You've got to make sure your head is on straight. Lara needs you to use your head right now. Your heart will make decisions later. Clear?"

He looked into his dad's eyes. He *did* know how Tate felt. His mom had been lost for a time back in the day.

"Yeah. It's hard."

"I know."

Aidyn was waiting for them by the door as they entered.

"We're ready."

"Thanks Aid. I appreciate it."

Stepping further into the house, his teammates were all there. Geared up and ready to roll. He nodded at them and had to take a deep breath to get his emotions under control.

When he let it out, he nodded at his friends. "Thanks for being here for me."

Maya chuckled. "As if we wouldn't. Let's go get our baker."

Okay. He handed Maya the thumb drive. "This will kill the worm. You and Addy need to slip into the computer shed and insert this."

"Will do."

He turned to Spencer. "You on the computer tonight?"

"Yep. I'll be back in action soon."

Tate shook his head. "Just heal up. Someone needs to be on the computers to keep track of us. Mom will help you watch."

Spencer grinned and looked at his mom. "Sounds good."

He turned to Henry and his dad. "When we get halfway up the hill we need to separate. You two go west, Aidyn and I will go east. I suspect he has her in Everett's cabin."

Using his phone he pulled a map up and showed them a general area where Everett's cabin was located. "They have houses all around. The computer cabin is in this area." He pointed to the spot near the road closest to the base. "They'll likely be watching us." He pointed between his dad, Henry, Aidyn, and himself. "Maya and Addy, you should be able to slip up there nearly undetected. But be wary; they seem to be everywhere. I'm sure they'll be expecting us."

Maya nodded then turned to Addy. She grinned. "We've got this."

He looked at his team, then his parents. "Okay. Let's go. We've only got an hour."

He and Aidyn drove to the east side of town and found a spot behind a house where they parked their car. His father and Henry were behind them. Maya and Addy drove to the base to park.

Silently making their way across the street, they started up the black road, stopping a hundred yards before it ended. It didn't get them even to halfway, but it was easier going than moving through the woods.

At that point, they turned on their comm units and slid into the duskiness of the wooded terrain. He looked back at his dad and Henry and nodded as they parted ways.

The path they took was a combination of rocks jutting out from brush and dead branches and soil made soft and murky from lack of sunlight. They had infrared goggles, but it wasn't quite dark and discerning the soil from the rocks while not losing their balance tested their patience.

They moved back and forth a few hundred feet to remain undetected. Aidyn stopped at a tree where a basket laid. He looked at the basket, found it empty, and kept moving.

Movement ahead of them halted their progress. They knelt and listened. Low voices sounded through the woods. Most of the conversation was difficult to hear. Some of it, though, made his blood run cold.

"If he doesn't follow through tonight, you know what to do."

"I do."

"Don't hesitate. Don't wimp out."

"I won't."

Their steps faded as one of them moved across the mountain to the east. The other one moved up toward the top.

Tate looked back at Aidyn and pointed to the top of the mountain, and Aidyn nodded. They gave themselves a bit of time before continuing up the hill.

After hiking more than a mile, they neared a clearing and hunkered down to watch. There was a group of women, sitting around a fire, stirring various bowls of something. The little bowls were situated close to the fire, as if they were melting something. They'd walk from bowl to bowl and stir. When it appeared a bowl had melted enough, they picked it up with hot pads or material and slowly carried it to a larger kettle across the clearing. It was slowly poured into that kettle, one person stirring the large kettle with a long paddle.

A man walked out of a shelter near the large kettle. "How much longer?"

"Not long. About five more minutes and it'll be ready to distill."

The first man turned toward a line of shelters and yelled. "Get ready to haul. Five minutes."

People began scrambling around, picking up tin pots and old coffee pots. It all looked like camping gear. Their clothing was a myriad of hand-me-down looking clothes. Some men wore jeans, likely stolen from the townies. He'd heard the stories of residents missing their laundry from the clotheslines. Most of them had stopped drying their clothes outside because of this.

Others wore long cloaks or long dress-like clothes that reached the ground. On their feet, some wore sandals, others wore old tennis shoes or boots. Again, all looked well-worn. Their hair was fashioned in intricate braids and twists and from what it seemed, those tending their elixir were dressed slightly better than those on the perimeter carrying whatever was in the bowls, and those who were now lined up to carry the concoction in the large kettle to the distillery.

A small, delicate looking woman, who seemed to be in her late twenties or early thirties, studied the concoction in the kettle and stirred it with the paddle. She lifted the paddle and watched as the brew dripped from it, then shook her head and pointed to the containers the other people carried.

Several more of them lined up, slowly pouring the contents of their containers into the kettle as the little woman stirred. Her dark hair was pulled back in a ponytail at her nape and trailed down her back. Aidyn whispered, "That's the woman we saw the other night."

Tate focused on her and nodded. "Yep."

She stirred a bit more. Repeating her motions, she lifted the paddle and then nodded to the man standing close by.

"It's ready," the man yelled.

A younger man ran toward the kettle with an old, dented trumpet and blew the horn in a series of long and short notes.

Everett walked toward the kettle. His long white hair was twisted and braided in intricate patterns. He wore long white pants that hid any shape or size. He had on a matching shapeless shirt. It reminded Tate of the uniform worn by doctors and nurses—scrubs. Over the top of his scrubs, he wore the pelt made of what looked like a wolf. They attached the tail at the back, and it hung down close to the ground.

As the man neared the kettle, the people bowed to him.

He held his hands out over the kettle and said a few quiet words.

A group of men, dressed similarly, though not in white, stood alongside him, but they didn't bow. The second man behind Everett also had long intricate braids and items woven into his hair. "I'd bet the man in the black scrubs is Craig Howard. Next in line."

"Yep."

Aidyn whispered. "Everett Howard is treated like a king. That must be his posse standing with him."

"I believe you're right."

He looked around for Kent and didn't see him. He whispered in his comm unit, "We don't see Kent, though they are preparing for a ceremony. Eyes up."

Everett Howard stood back and nodded. The hill folks then proceeded one by one to fill their containers and walk them to the shelter where he could see a still inside. They poured their liquid into the still and walked back for more.

It was a good time for exploration, while they were involved in their ritual.

FORTY-FIVE

Lara watched as the older woman prepared a dress made of cotton material and adorned with stitching in intricate patterns on the bodice. It was shapeless and white, and it made her stomach tighten.

The old woman hummed as she worked. She laid a sheet on the table, then moved the dress to lay on top of the sheet. She had an old metal iron that looked like something used in the early part of the nineteen hundreds. She heated it on the wood stove, then turned to press wrinkles from the dress.

"What's your name?"

The woman's old eyes looked into hers and her lips pressed together. "I'm Faye."

"Faye, please help me leave here. I don't want to marry Everett. I don't even know him. Anything my father has done is his burden to bear, not mine."

Faye stared for a long time then continued pressing the wrinkles from the dress. "Do you even know what your father's sins are, Lara?"

"No. Not completely."

Faye warmed the iron on the wood stove once more, then turned and pressed the dress again. "My son is Kent." Faye lifted the iron and stared at her directly. Lara's heartbeat sped up, her mouth went dry as her mind reeled from what she was thinking.

"Is my father Kent's father?"

Faye's eyes watered. She took a deep breath and pressed the dress. "He is. I loved him so much."

Lara tried swallowing. "Did he know all along that Kent was his?"

"Yes. We saw each other regularly in those days."

"How old..." The words stuck in her throat. She took a breath, "How old is Kent?"

"He's twenty-five."

So, for at least twenty-six years her father lived a secret life. Up here. In the hills while she and her mother were down below. A tear trickled down her cheek as she remembered all the times her father was gone. Her mother said he was working. It was plausible when she was younger. But when she asked questions, they both shut her down.

Faye moved to warm the iron again then turned to watch her. "Your mother is a drug addict. She found herself some elixir when you were about three or four. She liked how she felt and that started a pattern that has continued to this day. Your father would come up here to trade for elixir. He traded money and supplies." She looked at the iron. "Things we could use."

Ironing once more she seemed mesmerized by finally telling her story. "I met him on one of his forays up here. He was so handsome and I was enthralled with being involved with a townie. He was forbidden and delicious.

But Everett, and his father before him, allowed it because I could get us things we needed. Then I got pregnant."

She bit her bottom lip. "Keaton wasn't very happy about it at first. But, in his way, I think he loved me. But he loved your mother more."

She sniffed and returned the iron to the stove. Picking up the dress, she laid it on the bed then swept across the room, so lightly she could be a dancer. A pair of shoes were tucked in a trunk. They were also white. Faye carried them to the sink and began rubbing the shoes with a cloth.

"He loved Laylah more than me. I was so embarrassed. So stupid. But he kept coming up here to see me once or twice a week. And as my belly grew..." She laid her hand on her tummy. "His gifts to me were grander." She pulled a silver chain from under her dress and held it up for Lara to see. "He bought me this silver heart. I never take it off."

She tucked it back inside her dress and laid her hand over where it rested for a moment before taking a deep breath and continuing with cleaning the shoes. "He brought me a wood stove for my cabin so Kent and I would be warm. He'd come up and chop wood sometimes to help me when Kent was too little to help. A lot of the folks up here didn't want to help me. I didn't fit in. I had a bastard with a townie. I was tainted."

Her lips tipped up at the corners slightly and she shrugged. "But I could supply them with things, so they had to help me a little bit."

Lara nodded. It explained so much of her father's behaviors. The secrets. The absences. Her mother's avoidance of contact with her. She swallowed as the emotions rushed her. Her mom wasn't able to love because she was likely high all the time. As Lara grew older, she would just take off and hang at Shianne's all the time. It made sense now.

"Thank you."

Faye turned to her and stared. "Thank you? Why are you thanking me?"

"It explains so many of the questions I've always had growing up. Why my father wasn't around. Why my mother was often alone in her bedroom. Why she was always sick."

Faye nodded. "He felt responsible to keep her from crashing. He enabled her. I enabled him because it made him come up here for more elixir. We had a pattern."

"Why did it change this year?"

Faye shook her head. "The mayor and the town council stopped the tax deferment. Keaton said he couldn't pay more for the elixir. Supplies weren't good enough anymore because Everett needed the money. Keaton promised to sell the elixir to other communities and then he reneged and failed to sell it. Everett cut him off from the elixir. I understand your mother isn't taking it well."

Lara's eyes shot to Faye's. She knew everything. "Why does Kent hate me?"

She laughed and shook her head. "He has some stupid notion that you have what he doesn't. Keaton paid for him to go off to college. I hated that. We fought about that a lot. But, Kent is smart and he wanted to learn how to work on computers of all things. He has a crazy notion he can make our lives better up here. Then Keaton lied to us and refused to sell, and Kent sees you down there in your pretty bakery, with your own business. Keaton stops in to see you often and that makes Kent so mad."

Lara shook her head. "I have nothing to do with Kent's situation or his life. I've been in the dark all this time."

Faye shrugged. "He doesn't see it that way."

FORTY-SIX

Tate and Aidyn moved to the back of Everett's cabin. Aidyn watched the ceremony near the center of the grounds and Tate slowly rose to look in a window. He saw Lara tied to a chair across the room. An older woman tended to a pair of shoes at the sink, which was only a basin of water and a counter.

Lara had something on her face and tried wiping it on her shoulders. The woman moved to her with a fresh cloth and dabbed her face.

She made several trips to the basin then to Lara. But to his relief, he could see she was gentle with Lara.

Aidyn tapped him and pointed down. He fell to the ground, and they moved away from the cabin and toward the woods. He moved around to the opposite side of the cabin where he could see the center of the grounds. Everett strode toward the cabin. He whispered in his comm unit. "She's in Everett's house. Tied to a chair."

His dad responded quietly. "It's fifteen minutes to six."

Tate swallowed and scooted closer to the cabin to

hear what Everett was saying; he peered into a side window.

Everett turned to Lara and nodded. "You'll be my wife in a few minutes Lara. You'll be mine to do with as I please. If I have to keep you tied to that chair for all of your life, I'll do it." To the old woman, he said, "Have her ready in five minutes. The elixir is nearly ready and people are gathering in the circle."

He saw the tears slide down Lara's face. Then a commotion outside drew Everett's attention and he stomped from the cabin. Aidyn whispered in the comm unit. "Keaton is here making a scene."

There was only one door to get into the cabin, so he was going to need to slip in quickly. "I'm going in."

"I'll watch out here."

Glancing around the corner of the cabin, he saw Keaton and Everett in an argument. Keaton stepped forward. Craig Howard punched him in the face and Keaton went down hard. The people closed in the circle and Tate took that moment to slip into the cabin.

He heard someone yell, "Intruder." So he pulled a large dresser near the door in front of it as a barricade.

He turned to Lara and saw her tears. The older woman watched him closely as he went behind Lara to untie her hands.

He struggled with the knots and saw he was making the abrasions on her wrists bleed. He clamped his jaw together tightly and pulled out his knife. "Don't move, baby." She whimpered and the old woman took a step toward them. "Don't take another step. I will shoot you."

She froze.

Lara asked, "What's going on outside?"

"Craig is beating the shit out of your father."

The woman gasped and ran to the door. She shoved and pushed at the dresser enough to get through and the instant she disappeared out the door a shot rang out.

The crowd outside began yelling and screaming and another shot rang out.

Aidyn's voice snapped through the comm unit. "We don't have much time."

"We're on our way out."

"Go out the window. We'll meet you there."

Tate pulled her by the hand to the window at the back of the cabin. Henry and his father were running toward the cabin as he pushed the window open. He lifted Lara and tucked her through the window feet first for his dad to catch her. He followed closely behind as another shot was heard.

His dad yelled, "Out now. Down the hill."

They ran as fast as they could. The terrain was rugged but he helped Lara and she did rather well on her own. Each time they heard a gunshot she jerked but kept going. Her tears ran down her face, breaking his heart for her, but she didn't stop.

Footfalls behind them spurred them on. Henry stepped off to the side at one point and yelled, "Keep going. I'll give you some time."

Aidyn stepped off to the opposite side and huffed out. "Same. Go."

Lara tripped and he tightened his grip on her hand and pulled her up. They slowed only slightly. Once the road was paved, they moved to the road and ran down as fast as they could.

Maya and Addy called out. "We're done. On our way down."

Through their comm units he heard Henry and Aidyn

in a fight; the thuds of fists and the grunts as they hit the ground were unmistakable.

As they reached the bottom of the road his dad took off at a sprint across the road and soon came barreling across the road in the old Impala, screeching to a halt alongside them. Tate practically pushed Lara into the back seat then jumped in behind her. His dad stepped on the gas and they drove up the road as fast as they could. He told Henry and Aidyn, "We're on our way up the road in the Impala, get ready to jump in. Aidyn up front, Henry in the back."

He pulled Lara toward him in the middle of the car and his dad hit the brakes hard. The car barely stopped before the doors were wrenched open. His dad put the car in reverse and before the doors were closed, they were backing down the hill. No one said a word for a long time.

Maya finally said, "Addy and I are in the car on our way home."

He heaved out a breath and for the first time, Lara sobbed.

He put his arm around her and pulled her close, but his eyes were on the hills and surrounding area as were his teammates.

When they reached the road at the bottom of the hill, his dad pulled into the parking area and pulled his keys from his pocket and reached them over to Aidyn. Henry opened his door as well, "I'll ride with Aidyn."

Lara sniffed. "Who was shot?"

Aidyn heard her through the comm unit. "Everett."

"My dad?" She asked.

"I couldn't see him."

She nodded. "What about Faye?"

He looked at her, his eyebrows rose. "She is Kent's mom. She told me all about her and my dad."

He nodded and Aidyn sighed. "She was shot too. One of them shot her."

Lara sniffed. Then looked out the windshield. "There's going to be a war."

FORTY-SEVEN

Tate's mom helped him put his tux jacket on. He'd promised Lara they'd go to the ball. And after all the commotion of the past week, he was damned sure going to show up there. His entire team. He knew she didn't care that much, but after her father's funeral and her mom sent off to rehab, she needed something to be normal. And, he wanted to see her in her dress.

His mom brushed the invisible lint from his shoulders, and he turned slowly to hug her. "You look beautiful. I'm glad you and dad decided to join us."

"It was rather hard saying no to Shianne. That girl is a force."

"That she is."

His dad entered the room and chuckled. "I never dreamed I'd be going to a formal ball when we agreed to come down here."

Tate laughed. "It was the last thing I expected too."

They exited the bedroom and waited in the living room for Lara. She dressed in their bedroom alone. She wanted to surprise him. Why not let her have some fun? She'd been through an emotional rollercoaster this week.

He stood near the kitchen door. He didn't want to get his slacks wrinkled. After all the instructions from Shianne, he half joked they should just walk to the ball.

The bedroom door opened and he turned to see Lara glide down the hall. She looked magnificent. The gown flowed around her like a princess dress. Her words, not his. But now he saw what she meant. Shouldn't every girl feel like a princess some time in her life?

He tapped his pocket, checking that he had all he needed. Her lip gloss, her powder, and the tickets. But his eyes never left hers.

He stepped toward her and held his hands out to her. The instant she touched him, he felt the electricity flow through them both. He hoped he never lost that feeling.

"You're the most beautiful woman in the world."

His dad chuckled and his cheeks flamed. Tate turned to his mom. "You know what I mean."

His dad pulled his mom in for a hug. "I think you're the most beautiful woman in the world."

He shrugged at Lara and kissed her lips. "Stunning. You take my breath away."

"You are the most handsome man in the world." He kissed her again, then turned and held his arm out for her to take. The four of them walked outside to the waiting limousine.

He helped Lara slide in with all her layers, then he stiffly sat and moved over for his parents. The driver opened a bottle of champagne and poured them each a glass. He held his high. "I'd like to toast the Vickers family." He turned to Lara. "Which you are now part of."

His mom giggled, and they tapped glasses. The ride

was brief. Porter's Steakhouse was the host, and the drive was only ten miles.

Lara thanked his mom. "I appreciate your help today, Sophie. I wouldn't have finished all the cookies in time without you." Tate laughed. "Mom doesn't cook. She can kick someone's ass, but she doesn't cook."

Sophie shrugged. "Lara was patient with me and finally settled on having me wait on customers while she baked. That was the magic bullet. She finished with hours to spare."

They pulled into Porter's and Aidyn pulled in behind them.

"Lara and Sophie, you'll be the envy of the ball. I'll help you fight off suitors."

Lara shook her head and giggled. His mom rolled her eyes then Aidyn got serious and lowered his voice. "I saw her again today. I think she's following me."

"Who?"

"Elena." He looked around. "The dark-haired woman from the mountain. She came down the mountain and stopped to watch me. She carried her basket and as I drove past, she made a point of setting it down near a tree. Then she covered it with vines."

"She disappears like the wind when she wants. I turned around and went back to see what was in the basket. She had left a note that said, 'Hi.'"

"Just, 'Hi?'"

"Yes. I think it's her way of feeling things out."

"What are you going to do about it?"

Aidyn rubbed his jaw and shrugged. "I'm going to leave her a note and ask if we can have a chat."

"Why?"

"I like her. She's interesting and I don't think she's

like the others. Plus, she helped us get out of there when the shooting started. She pointed and nodded to the cabin to warn me Everett was near."

"Truth."

They neared the door to the steakhouse, and he leaned forward slowly and held it open for Lara. He winked at her when she passed him. His hand immediately found a home on her back. They stepped into the ballroom, all decorated in crepe paper and all things Bourbon. Barrels, corks, bottles. All of it tastefully done. The band was playing and he whispered near Lara's ear, "Would you like to dance with me?"

She turned her head. The most beautiful smile he'd ever seen was on her lips and she nodded. "I'd love nothing more."

He laughed as he took her hand and led her to the dance floor. The goal was to hold her tight and whisper beautiful words in her ears. And show the townspeople she was not her father.

"I love you, Lara."

She giggled. "I love you, Tate."

"I want to be your date every year for this ball."

She giggled again. "Okay. You'll have to ask before anyone else does, though."

He stopped twirling her around the dance floor and stopped them in the middle. He got down on one knee. Something he'd practiced this week.

"I'm asking for the rest of my life if you'll be my date for the Bourbon Ball and all dances? Will you marry me? Bear my children? Through sickness and in health? Will you be my wife?"

The crowd stopped and stared; the music stopped,

and Lara smiled the most radiant smile he'd ever seen. "I'd love nothing more."

His heart galloped; his breathing came in shallow spurts as he slid the ring on her finger, then stood. He kissed her lips, then whooped. "She said yes!"

The band played a quick wedding march and applause thundered around them. Shianne ran over. "Oh, my God. I can't believe I just saw that, Lara." She wrapped Lara in a bear hug. "Congratulations."

She lunged at him, and he grimaced before letting her hug him.

"You better treat my bestie right."

"I promise."

His parents and his teammates were next, and all he remembered was that Lara said yes.

***

Tate and Lara are about to get married and you're invited to witness their big day. Click here to attend the wedding.

AIDYN IS ENAMORED WITH ELENA, but they're from two very different worlds. In her world, Aidyn is the enemy, in his, she brings danger. Find out if Aidyn can Save Elena.

Saving Elena

ALSO BY PJ FIALA

You can find all of my books at https://pjfiala.com/books

Romantic Suspense

Rolling Thunder Series

Moving to Love, Book 1

Moving to Hope, Book 2

Moving to Forever, Book 3

Moving to Desire, Book 4

Moving to You, Book 5

Moving On, Book 6

Rolling Thunder Boxset 1, Books 1-3

Rolling Thunder Boxset 2, Books 4-6

Military Romantic Suspense

Second Chances Series

Designing Samantha's Love, Book 1

Securing Kiera's Love, Book 2

Bluegrass Security Series

Heart Thief, Book One

Finish Line, Book Two

Lethal Love, Book Three

Wrenched Fate, Book Four

Lynyrd Station Protectors - Security

Finding His Fire Book One

Finding His Mark Book Two

Finding His Jewel Book Three

Finding His Match Book Four

Lynyrd Station Protectors Boxset, Books 1-3

GHOST

Defending Keirnan, GHOST Book One

Defending Sophie, GHOST Book Two

Defending Roxanne, GHOST Book Three

Defending Yvette, GHOST Book Four

Defending Bridget, GHOST Book Five

Defending Isabella, GHOST Book Six

GHOST Box Set One (Books 1-3)

GHOST Box Set Two (Books 4-6)

RAPTOR

RAPTOR Rising - Prequel

Saving Shelby, RAPTOR Book One

Holding Hadleigh, RAPTOR Book Two

Craving Charlesia, RAPTOR Book Three

Promising Piper, RAPTOR Book Four

Missing Mia, RAPTOR Book Five

Believing Becca, RAPTOR Book Six

Keeping Kori, RAPTOR Book Seven

Healing Hope, RAPTOR Book Eight

Engaging Emersyn, RAPTOR Book Nine

RAPTOR Box Set 1

RAPTOR Box Set 2

RAPTOR Box Set 3

GHOST Legacy (Next generation)

Finding Lara, Book One

Saving Elena, Book Two

Rescuing Kenna, Book Three

Protecting Everleigh, Book Four

Guarding Adelaide, Book Five

Shielding Maya, Book Six

ENJOY THIS BOOK? YOU CAN MAKE A BIG DIFFERENCE

Reviews are the most powerful tools in my arsenal when it comes to getting attention for my books. As much as I'd like to, I don't have the financial muscle of a New York publisher. I can't take out full page ads in the newspaper or put posters on the subway.

(Not yet, anyway.)

But I do have something much more powerful and effective than that, and it's something that those big publishers would die to get their hands on.

A committed and loyal bunch of readers.

Honest reviews of my books help bring them to the attention of other readers.

If you've enjoyed this book I would be so grateful to you if you could spend just five minutes leaving a review (it can be as short as you like) on the book's vendor page. You can jump right to the page of your choice by clicking below.

Thank you so very much.

MEET PJ

Writing has been a desire my whole life. Once I found the courage to write, life changed for me in the most profound way. Bringing stories to readers that I'd enjoy reading and creating characters that are flawed, but lovable is such a joy.

When not writing, I'm with my family doing something fun. My husband, Gene, and I are bikers and enjoy riding to new locations, meeting new people and generally enjoying this fabulous country we live in.

I come from a family of veterans. My grandfather, father, brother, two sons, and one daughter-in-law are all veterans. Needless to say, I am proud to be an American and proud of the service my amazing family has given.

My online home is https://www.pjfiala.com.
You can connect with me on Facebook at https://www.facebook.com/PJFiala1,
and
Instagram at https://www.Instagram.com/PJFiala.
If you prefer to email, go ahead, I'll respond - pjfiala@pjfiala.com.

Printed in the United States of America

First published 2022

Fiala, PJ

FINDING LARA / PJ Fiala

p. cm.

1. Romance—Fiction. 2. Romance—Suspense. 3. Romance - Military

I. Title – FINDING LARA

ISBN-13: 978-1-959386-34-6